Emily Harvale lives in Eas
although she would prefer
Alps…or Canada…or anywhere that has several
months of snow. Emily loves snow almost as much
as she loves Christmas.

Having worked in the City (London) for several
years, Emily returned to her home town of
Hastings where she spends her days writing. And
wondering if it will snow.

You can contact her via her website, Twitter,
Facebook, Instagram or Pinterest.

Author contacts:
www.emilyharvale.com
www.twitter.com/emilyharvale
www.facebook.com/emilyharvalewriter
www.facebook.com/emilyharvale
www.pinterest.com/emilyharvale
www.instagram.com/emilyharvale

***

Scan the code above to see all Emily's books on
Amazon

Also by this author:

Highland Fling
Lizzie Marshall's Wedding
The Golf Widows' Club
Sailing Solo
Carole Singer's Christmas
Christmas Wishes – Two short stories
A Slippery Slope
The Perfect Christmas Plan – A novella
Be Mine – A novella
***

The Goldebury Bay series:
Book One – Ninety Days of Summer
Book Two – Ninety Steps to Summerhill
Book Three – Ninety Days to Christmas
***

The Hideaway Down series:
Book One – A Christmas Hideaway
Book Two – Catch A Falling Star
Book Three – Walking on Sunshine
Book Four – Dancing in the Rain
***

Hall's Cross series
Deck the Halls
The Starlight Ball

The Starlight Ball

Emily Harvale

ISBN 978-1-909917-22-4

Published by Crescent Gate Publishing

Print edition published worldwide 2017
E-edition published worldwide 2017

Editor Christina Harkness

Cover design by JR, Luke Brabants and Emily Harvale

This book is dedicated to my dear friend, Joanna.
Remember, Jo, wishes can come true.

Acknowledgements

My special thanks go to the following:

Christina Harkness for editing this book.
Christina's input is much appreciated.
My webmaster, David Cleworth who does so
much more than website stuff.
My cover design team, JR.
Luke Brabants. Luke is a fabulous artist and can
be found at: www.lukebrabants.com
My wonderful friends for their support and
friendship. You know I love you all.
My Twitter and Facebook friends, and fans of
my Facebook author page. It's great to chat with
you. You help to keep me (relatively) sane!
And to you, for buying this book. Thank You.

The Starlight Ball

Wishes can come true

Chapter One

On reflection, organising an afternoon tea party and inviting the two hundred or so residents of Hall's Cross, together with half the surrounding villages, is possibly not one of my best ideas. Especially a mere few weeks before my fifty-year-old stepmum, Bella is due to give birth. And possibly not in May. After several days of rain, perhaps I should have cancelled. But English weather is changeable, to say the least, and I was sure it would change for the better. Which it did. For a short while. But maybe I should have listened to my great-aunt.

'You've heard the saying, Harriet,' Aunt Vicki warned me. 'I have said it often enough. "Cast ne'er a clout till May be out" – which means one should definitely *not* plan outdoor functions in May.'

'This is England, Aunt.'

'I am well aware of that. I may be ninety next month but I am not senile.'

That came as a bit of a surprise. Not the senile bit – her age. I thought she was ninety, years ago. She looks like that Dowager Countess from the *Downtown Abbey* TV series and has done for as long as I can remember. The only difference is that Aunt Vicki's dresses are slightly shorter and she would never be seen dead using a cane.

'I know you're not.' I pretended to ignore the 'ninety' part. Although I did wonder if she said that for a reason. Ninety is a pretty big deal. Maybe she wanted to remind me in case Dad and Bella forget to do something special to celebrate. Bella's due date is in June, so it'll be a month of celebrations at this rate. 'What I meant was, we were all lounging in deckchairs in March.'

'It snowed at Easter.'

'True. But the temperature has been hovering around 18 degrees for the last few days.'

'After two weeks of rain.'

'It'll be fine. And if it does rain, we can simply move all the animals indoors.'

'Indoors! In...doors! Good heavens, Harriet. You are surely not suggesting we turn The Hall into some sort of Ark?'

'Of course I'm not. The animals can be moved into the stables, with Pegasus and Sirius.'

Aunt Vicki loves The Hall, possibly more than she does her relatives. It has been the ancestral home of the Hall family since the late fifteenth century, but it's not as grand as it sounds. It's really an extended Tudor manor house which, until late last year, was falling down around my family's ears. The estate includes several acres of parkland and woods and sits at the edge of the village of Hall's Cross and it takes a large fortune to keep up a place like this. We don't even possess a small fortune, so it has been tough, to say the least. And Pegasus and Sirius are our somewhat ancient horse and equally ancient donkey. They share the seventeenth-century stable block with several old rust-bucket cars. And I do mean *rust-buckets*. There are no Ferraris or Bentleys or such amongst our collection of vehicles.

'And what about Bella?'

I couldn't help but smile. 'Oh, I think we can let Bella into the house, don't you?'

Aunt Vicki tried to pretend she didn't find that funny, but I saw her wafer-thin lips curve a fraction before she snapped at me.

'That is not in the least bit amusing, child. Your stepmother is about to give birth. Surely this scheme of yours can wait?'

'Bella's not due for a few more weeks, and besides, I've discussed it with her. She's fine with it. You worry too much, Aunt.'

'I have a great deal to worry about, living in this madhouse. This will not end well, Harriet, but it is clear that your mind is made up and you will not listen to reason.' Aunt Vicki turned and marched away. For an almost-ninety-year-old, she's still quite sprightly, when she wants to be, that is. 'Mark my words,' she said, turning back to look at me before shoving the kitchen door open with considerable force. 'I can feel it in my bones. This has disaster written all over it. Reece? Where are you, boy? I think it's high time I had a cocktail.' The door swung shut behind her and that was the last she said about it.

I should have listened, of course. But I didn't. And to be honest, Bella did have one or two reservations about the whole thing; until I assured her that there was really nothing to worry about and the afternoon would go off without so much as a tiny hitch.

As I stand here, surrounded by what Aunt Vicki has said are my "just desserts", I make a mental note. In future, Harriet Hall, listen to your elders.

But it's too late to do that now.

I meant well, of course. I always do. My stepsister, Merrion is constantly telling me that I suffer from unbridled optimism. Which is true. I firmly believe things will turn out perfectly well, no matter what. Even when they don't, as is often the case, I can still find a sliver of silver in any clouds sent to rain on my parade.

This time though, even I'm struggling to see a ray of hope.

The sole purpose of this event was to help swell the coffers of the Hall's Cross Animal Rescue Sanctuary and now I'll be lucky if they don't get sued by one of our guests. Although I suppose the guests would probably sue me and my family rather than the sanctuary. I don't suppose anyone will open their cheque books or hand over wads of cash, in any case, which is a real pity because the sanctuary needs all the help it can get.

Well okay. Adding cash to the sanctuary's meagre funds wasn't the *only* reason I wanted to hold the event. I'm actually trying to sort out the love lives of various members of my family, and my boyfriend Lance's younger sister, Gwen.

It still gives me such a thrill to use the words 'my boyfriend' and 'Lance' in the same sentence. Lance Knightly is the most gorgeous, wonderful, sexy man in the entire world – and he's *my* boyfriend. We've been together since Christmas Eve. That's a whole five months. Almost. Give or take a couple of weeks. But who's counting weeks when Lance and I will be spending the rest of our lives together? Oh. I suppose, technically, I am.

But right now I watch as if I've been glued to the spot, as a particularly scruffy-looking Irish wolfhound, deposits a steaming pile of poo on the once-gleaming polished oak floor of the Great Hall.

'Another dog's just…' Merrion glances at me with a definite *I'm not clearing it up* look on her face, but she doesn't need to finish her sentence.

'I can see that.'

I shouldn't snap at her I know, but frankly, stating the obvious isn't helping. This is the third dog that's done 'his business' inside the house and two others have peed. One of them even used one of the ornate newel posts at the foot of the stairs as a makeshift tree. Those posts are centuries old and have large Grecian urns atop them, which I always think may topple off until I remind myself they're part of the design and were carved into shape by hand. To say that Dad isn't pleased to see such superb craftsmanship being piddled on by a dog is an understatement of huge proportions.

I feel I should be doing something useful to help instead of simply standing here, watching the chaos. But Lance told me to stay exactly where I was and my stepbrother Ralph said that I'd already done enough. And I don't think he meant that in a good way. So I'm staying put. So is Merrion. And so is Aunt Vicki, who is leaning back in one of the winged chairs, trying to look both annoyed and disgusted at the same time. But I've seen a smile curve her wrinkle-feathered lips, and her frail-looking shoulders have shaken more than once since this mayhem kicked off. I'm assuming that's because she's trying to stifle laughter... but I could be wrong. After all, it may look amusing if someone filmed this and sent it to one of those 'funny videos' TV shows, but not many of our guests are laughing and I'm definitely struggling to see anything funny about any of this at the moment. Merrion, who looks drop-dead gorgeous as always with her blonde hair and designer-labelled, red silk dress, did burst out laughing a few minutes ago, but a look from Dad put a stop to that. She's standing one side of Aunt Vicki, beside me and my other stepbrother, fifteen-year-old, Reece. Bella is seated in a matching winged chair opposite Aunt Vicki, and Dad is holding her hand, reassuringly, I assume. Although I'm not sure who is reassuring whom. Dad hasn't moved an inch. He's just watched, like me, with his eyes wide and his mouth gaping open.

'Who let the dogs out?' Reece asks, pushing his glasses back into position on his nose, with the tip of one finger.

I half expect him to start humming and barking, but this is Reece, and he's a bit of a chemistry nerd. He's completely unaware of any similarity between his question and the title of the well-known pop song. Reece doesn't listen to music – unless it's of the classical variety. I can't help but wonder sometimes how he gets through his days at the local school without getting beaten up by the village hoodlums. Perhaps it's because he's so good at blowing things up. Maybe the would-be bullies are a bit wary of upsetting him. Or perhaps they want to be in Reece's good books. They may want to enlist his services one day in the not too distant future to gain unauthorised entry to a bank vault or something. Or possibly my over-active imagination is running away with itself once again. To tell you the truth, I'm not even sure there are any hoodlums or bullies at Reece's school. I'm not even sure there are any in Hall's Cross, but as I lived in Australia for two years and have only been happily back in my family home since last

December, anything could have happened, I suppose. I haven't seen any during the last four and a half months, and the loan sharks and cowboy builders that Dad somewhat foolishly got involved with shortly after I went on my travels, all came from the vicinity of Newhaven. They haven't been back since Lance and Ralph apparently saw them off, thank goodness.

'We don't know for sure. And it isn't just the dogs that are out,' I reply, watching Lance, Ralph, the two staff from the sanctuary, and some of the villagers and other guests chasing the eight dogs, six cats, four rabbits, several chickens, three ducks, two goats and a tame fox that are currently running loose in The Hall and its grounds. 'But I have a good idea that the terrible twins had something to do with it.'

My half-brothers, Theo and Thor may only be four years old but they can cause more chaos than anyone would think is humanly possible. And they usually do. Shortly before the first muddy paws left their prints on the floor, we were all drinking tea, eating delicious pastries and cakes, and conversing amicably. That was obviously thoroughly boring for the twins. They had asked Bella if they could go and play with the animals, most of which were safely outside, either in large animal crates, allowing them to be easily viewed by any potential adopters, or held securely on leads by the two staff who accompanied them from the Hall's Cross Animal Rescue Sanctuary. Bella told the twins they must wait until we had finished tea and then we could all go and look at the delightful creatures. I suppose I should have known they weren't going to accept that. We all should have. Less than twenty minutes ago, Theo was sticking an iced bun onto the sword held by one of the two silver-plated armoured knights who've stood either side of the double front doors of The Hall for centuries. Thor was trying to balance a tea cup in the gauntlet of the other knight until Dad stopped him and told them both to try to behave.

Theo and Thor beamed up at him. 'Yes Daddy,' they said, as if butter wouldn't melt.

Dad ruffled their curly locks and told them to run along and that was the last time I saw them until a few minutes before several dogs came bounding into the Great Hall via the open front doors. I spotted Theo and Thor racing towards the dining room, trailing what looked suspiciously like a string of sausages. But I knew that couldn't be the case. After all, where on earth would they find a string of sausages? Then I remembered the village butcher had brought a large bag of fresh meat with him, which Dad had taken to the kitchen and no doubt put in the fridge or freezer. So now I'm absolutely convinced the twins must have got the sausages from the kitchen, sneaked outside via the kitchen garden and somehow managed to open all the crates before anyone realised what they were up to. Those two will grow up to be criminal masterminds, I'm sure of it.

To look at, they give the impression of two perfect little angels but believe me, they are far from angelic. Christmas was chaotic because of them. Well, not just because of them, but they caused the most havoc. New Year went with rather more of a bang than anyone expected, thanks to them. But come to think of it, that was as much Reece's fault as theirs, as yet another of his experiments, failed, this time involving homemade fireworks. The twins just added fuel to the flames... in more ways than one. And that meant, once the Fire Brigade had left, a small part of the west wing of The Hall had to be closed off for the entire month of January until Lance could make it safe and begin repairs. And by repairs, I mean serious rebuilding work. It's such a good thing that Lance owns his own building and renovation business. Dad was furious and tried, for the umpteenth time, to make Reece see how dangerous his experiments were, and for the twins to realise what they had done, but all Dad's words fell on deaf ears. I don't know what we would have done if it hadn't been for Lance. He took it all rather calmly, which was a little surprising as he and his team of builders had only finished fairly major renovation work on The Hall shortly before Christmas. But that's Lance for you. He takes everything in his rather sexy stride.

I can't help but smile as I think how wonderful Lance is, but it's soon wiped off my face.

'Look out!' Merrion's warning shout is too

late. Ralph and Lance career headlong into one another, landing in a tangled heap on the floor. The two dogs they had each been about to grab, nimbly dart out of harm's way and head in the direction of the kitchen.

'Don't let them get into the kitchen!' The look on Bella's face is one of sheer panic but as Dad's about to dash off in that direction she grabs his arm. 'Oh no.'

'I'll stop them,' Dad says, finally stirred into action by Bella's plea, and he gently tries to release her grip on his jacket.

Bella shakes her head. 'The dogs are the least of our worries, darling.' She looks down at her swollen belly and I feel my heart rate increase as I take in what's happening.

'But the baby's not due for another four weeks,' I mumble.

'All the excitement has brought this on.' Aunt Vicki tugs at the sleeve of my cashmere jumper; the one Lance bought me as a belated Christmas present, and she glares up at me. 'Well come along, child! Don't stand there like a buffoon. Help me up.'

Bella gives me a wane smile. 'Good heavens. Isn't this simply perfect timing? I'm so sorry about this, Harri.'

I'm struggling to get Aunt Vicki to her feet. She may be sparrow-like in frame but she's forceful in nature, and strangely enough, she's no featherweight. Getting her out of a chair is almost a Herculean task.

'I'm the one who should be sorry, Bella,' I say.

And from the looks Dad, Aunt Vicki, Merrion and… well everyone, actually, are giving me, I think I may be sorry for a long time to come.

Chapter Two

'That went well.' Merrion grins at me in her rear-view mirror. 'Have you got any more brilliant ideas for how to find Ralph, Gwen and me the loves of our lives? And if so, may I suggest you forget them. Immediately.'

'You knew! I mean… I don't know what you're talking about. It was to help the animals.'

I'm sitting in the back seat of Merrion's brand new Land Cruiser, as we're driving home from the hospital. She's only had it for two days and she's still getting used to it but I feel a lot safer in this than I did in her last car. She wrote that off a couple of weeks ago when she skidded off the road and into a ditch, on an exceedingly wet and blustery day. Thankfully, she walked away with only bruises, but Bella insisted that, unless Merrion wanted her mother to have a heart attack, its replacement should be something less sporty. Little does Bella know that this goes almost as fast as the Audi. At least it does with Merrion at the wheel.

'Yeah, right,' Merrion says. 'That's why several of the guests were single professionals between the ages of twenty-one to thirty. Of course I knew. Even Gwen has an inkling you're up to something and I'm certain Bella and Aunt Vicki guessed, as well as Lance. Ralph, naturally, is completely oblivious.'

Ralph's beside me, fast asleep, and Reece is intently studying some chemical formula or something on his iPad. Aunt Vicki is sitting in the front next to Merrion, and softly snoring. Lance, and his sister, Gwen, stayed on at The Hall. Lance told me to call him if I needed him, or when we knew for certain that the baby was coming. He felt that someone should remain behind until all the animals were safely back where they should be, and besides, the twins were still lurking somewhere and had to be found before they caused any further mischief.

As it happens, Bella wasn't going into labour. It seems it was a false alarm. But her blood pressure is high, for some reason, so the junior doctor they saw said she should spend the night and they'll see how she is in the morning. I suppose that might have something to do with what happened at the tea party, so technically, this is my fault and I feel awful.

No. Actually it's the terrible twins' fault. Everything would have gone smoothly if it hadn't been for those dreadful half-brothers of mine.

Merrion, Ralph and Gwen were having some very promising conversations with one or two of the guests and I know for certain two men asked for Merrion's number. What's more, some of those poor abandoned animals might have even found new homes. I wonder if we could afford to send Theo and Thor to a boarding school or something.

Dad stayed on at the hospital with Bella, but he insisted we should all go home. He also suggested we might like to make sure that all the mess is cleared up and that there are no semi-wild animals running riot so that when Bella does return, it'll be to a calm and pristine home, not a zoo. He was glaring at me when he said it. I know he loves me a great deal, but at that moment, I'm not sure he *liked* me very much.

I fix my gaze on Merrion's headrest. 'I'm only trying to help. It's about time you and Ralph both settled down. And Gwen needs to find someone to help her get over her ex. Lance is still so worried about her, you know.'

Merrion shakes her head. 'This is 2017, Harri, not the 1950s. People don't need to 'settle down'. It's perfectly okay for us to do what we want, when we want and with whomsoever we want without feeling the need to 'settle down'.'

'You know what I mean.'

'I know exactly what you mean, and that's the problem. I'm not sure Ralph will ever be ready to 'settle down', and I'm damned sure I won't. After living with my brothers Reece, Theo and Thor, there is no way I ever want kids. Ralph's okay but the odds are clearly against anyone in this family ever having well-behaved, normal offspring. I'm dreading what this next one will be like. God, I hope it's a girl. I wish they hadn't wanted to wait to see what it is. And as for Gwen, she's still only eighteen and she's already had one disastrous marriage. I don't think she's in any hurry to repeat that mistake and I'm pretty sure Lance would rather she remain single for some considerable time yet.'

'Na-huh. Lance told me himself just the other day that Gwen needs someone to look out for her.'

Merrion tuts. 'I think he meant himself. She needs someone to make sure she doesn't make the same mistake twice. Gwen's like you in many ways. An unbridled optimist, and a complete fool as far as love is concerned.'

'I'm not a fool! Are you saying that I'm making a mistake being madly in love with Lance?'

'No. Of course not. Although I do question the "madly" bit. But let's not forget that when you met Lance, you thought you were in love with Arthur Camlan-Brown. You even hoped he was going to propose to you at Christmas. And look how that turned out.'

'Yes. But as soon as I met Lance, I knew. I realised I didn't really love Art. Not the way you should if you're considering marriage.'

'Do you ever think of him and your life in

Australia?'

'Art? Once or twice. But not because I miss him or anything. And the only thing I miss about Sydney is the sun. It seemed so much brighter there somehow. But then I suppose I came home in the middle of winter and apart from those glorious sunny days in March, we haven't seen a lot of sunshine here. I thought I missed my clothes, and the few things of mine in the flat we shared, but when Art finally packed them up and had them shipped over, I realised none of them meant anything. Most of the stuff's still in the boxes it arrived in.'

Merrion sighs. 'Anyway, Harri. The point I was making is that you can't push people into love. And some people see love through rose-coloured glasses. You do. And Gwen does. Leave her to find her own way. What would happen to your relationship with Lance if you set Gwen up with someone and it turned into another nightmare? Do you think Lance would thank you for his baby sister going mental again?'

I shift uncomfortably in my seat. Merrion's got a point.

'I don't think Gwen went mental, exactly.'

'Hmm. I'm not sure Jackson Hunter would agree with you. And you weren't around when it happened. You've only heard about it from Lance. And he's not going to tell you his sister completely flipped her lid and got arrested, is he?'

'He told me she was arrested but the charges

were dropped. And when I asked you about it, you said it wasn't that bad.'

'I lied. I'm really fond of Lance… and Gwen, and I didn't want you rushing back to Lance and saying that I'd said his sister behaved like a raving loony and was bloody lucky that her husband didn't press charges. Gwen could have easily been locked up for what she did.'

'But Jackson behaved like a complete and utter shit. Gwen should never have married the jerk in the first place. Especially not on her seventeenth birthday. She had no idea what men were like. And she certainly wasn't equipped to deal with a man like Jackson bloody Hunter.'

'That's precisely my point. She still isn't.'

'She hasn't met the right man.'

'Oh, and you think you can find him, do you?'

'Yes.' I beam at her but thankfully she's focused on the road ahead. 'I re-read *Emma* a couple of weeks ago. You know, the book by Jane Austen. The one where she decides to be a matchmaker. And I thought how much fun that would be. Then I thought how wonderful it would be if you and Ralph could be as happy as I am. Then I thought about Gwen and… well… I decided I would be like Emma and try to fix you all up with the perfect partners.'

'You're insane.' Now she is looking at me. And there's a hint of concern in her vivid blue eyes. 'Look how that turned out. She made a complete mess of things. Besides, you're no Emma and this is *real* life.'

'I don't know what you mean by that. And you're wrong. Everyone found love. Well, almost everyone.'

'Not because of Emma's meddling.'

I ignore her remark. 'And I even have my own Mr Knightly.' I give her a rather smug smile. 'I hadn't realised that until the other day. That Lance has the same surname as one of Jane Austen's heroes. Isn't that amazing? What was his Christian name? I can't remember.'

'Who bloody cares! It certainly wasn't Lance, so the comparison ends there.' She shakes her head and sighs before returning her attention to her driving. 'It was George, I think. And Emma's Knightley has an 'e' in it. Your Knightly doesn't.'

'George? Was it? I thought it was something far more romantic than George. Are you sure about that?'

'About as sure as I am that you trying to organise other people's love lives will end in the same way as your delightful afternoon tea party did today. I dread to think about the mess we're going to find when we get home.'

'It wasn't my fault the dogs and all the other animals got out. And it certainly isn't my fault that it started blowing a gale the moment we left for the hospital.'

'I warned you several weeks ago.' Aunt Vicki's voice startles me. I thought she was fast asleep.

There's not much I can say. She did warn me and I didn't listen.

'I know you did. Perhaps I should have listened. But I meant well, Aunt, and if it hadn't been for the terrible twins, it would have been a perfect day.'

'Shit!' Merrion swerves to avoid a branch lying in the road leading into the village of Hall's Cross but she quickly regains control. 'It's getting really bad out there. Thank God we're almost home.'

Aunt Vicki and I nod silently as Merrion drives past the picture-postcard Tudor houses towards the massive ancient stone cross in the tiny village square and the equally antiquated pub, The Cross in Hand. Ralph's head flops onto my shoulder as we head towards the more modern Victorian terraced homes at the other end of the village. From here we can see the stone pillars either side of the drive leading to The Hall. Ralph's still sound asleep and I notice that Reece remains engrossed by his iPad.

It's getting dark now and it's hard to see through the torrential rain but something runs in front of Merrion's headlights as we turn into the drive. I only catch a glimpse but I'm sure it's that scruffy-looking Irish wolfhound that only a few short hours ago had kindly made a large and smelly deposit on the floor of the Great Hall. And that means Lance and the others still haven't caught all the escapees yet.

Yep. I'm definitely going to remember this day

for a very long time to come. And not in a good
way, that's for sure.

Chapter Three

Merrion parks at the foot of the steps leading up to the double doors of The Hall so that Aunt Vicki doesn't have far to walk in this dreadful weather. Ralph, who woke up the second Merrion switched off the engine, gets out and helps Aunt Vicki down. It's a bit of a step from the Land Cruiser to the ground and she takes his proffered arm, giving him a brief but grateful smile in return. There's no point in using an umbrella; it's far too windy, so Ralph lifts his jacket over her to shield her from the worst of the rain, just as a sudden gust of near-gale force wind almost blows her off her feet. He wraps an arm around her and, half carrying her hurries up the steps towards the doors and the shelter of the colonnade, where he deposits her safely on the stone floor. She reaches up and kisses his cheek and he shoves one of the doors open and helps her inside.

It still amazes me how much Aunt Vicki has mellowed during the years I was in Australia. I remember the days when she wouldn't give Ralph the time of day. Or any other man for that matter, including Dad, and he's her own nephew. Now she is sweetness and light to all. Most of the time. And Reece, who makes her various cocktails out of the most colourful, bubbling, concoctions you could ever hope to see, is definitely her favourite. Although having said that, my boyfriend Lance comes a very close second.

Speaking of Lance, here he is. He doesn't look particularly happy though as he and another man march towards Merrion, Reece and me, apparently unperturbed by the wind we three are struggling against. It's buffeting me to and fro and whipping my ginger-red hair all over my face. It's doing the same to Merrion and lifting her dress so high that she has to grab the hem with one hand whilst steadying herself against her car with the other. I'm glad I'm wearing trousers.

Even Reece is knocked off-balance as he moves towards the steps. 'Come on,' he says, turning back and stretching out his hands to me and Merrion but as he's having trouble remaining upright I'm not sure he can help us.

'We've got them,' Lance says, taking my arm and leading me forward.

I see the other man, who's as tall as Lance and almost as broad-shouldered but has close-cropped blond hair in contrast to Lance's black, wild locks. He strides to Merrion's side. Another rain-filled gust tugs at Merrion's red silk dress and blows it skyward, exposing her matching lace panties to the world. She lets out a little scream and the seriously good-looking stranger stops in his tracks, stares at her for a second then grabs her arm and unceremoniously drags her towards the steps. She catches my concerned look and returns it with a mixture of shock and total embarrassment, which is odd for Merrion. She doesn't usually care what anyone thinks of her.

Once we're all inside, Lance pushes the door shut and gives me an anxious look.

'How's Bella?'

'She's fine.' I shake some of the rainwater from my hair and clothes. My cashmere jumper clearly doesn't like rain and I wonder if it'll ever look quite the same again. We should have taken coats with us, but only Ralph was sensible enough to think of that. 'It was a false alarm. But they're keeping her in overnight due to high blood pressure. Dad's staying with her just in case. She's no spring chicken, after all.'

'She's not the only one with high blood pressure,' Aunt Vicki says.

She's sitting in the same chair she was earlier and I wonder why she didn't go into the sitting room where I can see that someone has lit the fire.

'I'm going up to bed,' she adds, answering my unspoken question. 'As soon as Reece fixes me a cocktail or two.'

'Go into the warm and get dry,' Lance tells her. 'We may need Reece to help us.'

'Where are the twins?' I ask.

Lance grins at me. 'Fast asleep in bed. It took some doing and they wanted their mum. I told them Bella had gone to see if their brother or sister was ready to come home and they wouldn't be allowed to meet him or her unless they behaved. Suddenly, they were as good as gold.'

'Really? That's a bribe we can use for a while yet then.'

'I don't suppose you've seen an Irish wolfhound running around anywhere, have you?' the man standing beside Merrion asks. His voice is deep, like Lance's but there's a hint of irritation in his tone.

'Yes.' Merrion glances up at him and her face turns crimson. 'I nearly ran it over as we came down the drive.'

The man looks down at her but doesn't answer right away. When he does, he sounds genuinely cross.

'It? His name is Balthazar and I hope you didn't hit him. I've heard you're a terrible driver.'

'I am not!' Merrion glowers at him. 'Who told you that?'

'Someone or other. I'd better go and find him.'

'You do that. I hope you don't drag him back here the way you dragged me up those steps.'

'Don't blame me because you can't walk in those ridiculously high heels.'

'Um. Excuse me,' I say before Merrion has a chance to respond. I'm somewhat surprised by this odd exchange. 'Who *are* you?'

'What?' He turns angry-looking eyes towards me. 'I'm the manager of Hall's Cross Animal Rescue Sanctuary. My staff called me after the animals escaped. Long after, unfortunately. Although I'm not sure 'escaped' is the accurate word for how they got out. It's pretty clear that someone opened the doors of their crates. I must go and find Balthazar. My name is Dan. Daniel Barker.'

He glances towards Merrion as he gives his name and I can't help but wonder why.

'Barker!' Merrion sneers. 'That's the perfect name for you.'

He completely ignores her and yanks one of the double front doors open. As he does so, a violent gust of wind sweeps in and lifts Merrion's dress to her waist.

'You did that on purpose,' she screams, her face now matching the colour of her dress as she tries to get a hold of the wayward silk.

Dan glances back at her. Looks her up and down and steps outside, slamming the door shut behind him without another word.

'What on earth was that all about?' I stare from Merrion to Lance. 'Is he really the manager of the sanctuary? I've never seen him before and he definitely wasn't the person I dealt with when I arranged the afternoon tea party.'

Lance shrugs. 'I haven't a clue. I only met the guy half an hour or so ago but I suppose he must

26

be. Once all the guests had gone and we were able to get the animals we'd caught back in their crates, we realised one was still missing. The two girls from the sanctuary called him and he was here within twenty minutes. We've been separately scouring the grounds for the missing dog ever since so we've hardly spoken more than a few words to one another. I'd better go and help him. Reece, will you join us? Where did Ralph go? We could use his assistance.'

'I'm here.' Ralph appears from the kitchen carrying a bottle of whisky in one hand and several glasses on a tray in the other. 'I thought this would warm us up.'

Aunt Vicki grins. 'Leave that with me, my boy. Your services are required elsewhere. You've got to see a man about a dog.'

'Huh?'

Lance pats him on the shoulder. 'One of the dogs is still loose, Ralph. We've got to find him before he does himself, or someone else, an injury. And definitely before he finds his way into the village.'

'Damn.' Ralph hands the bottle to Aunt Vicki and places the tray of glasses on a small table nearby, and then lifts the table together with the glasses and puts them beside her chair. 'Save some for me.'

'We'll come too,' I say, frowning at Merrion because she still hasn't answered my question.

'You speak for yourself,' she snaps. 'This

entire shambles was your idea. You invited that ignorant pig of a man into our house by organising this fiasco. You help if you like. I'm staying here with Aunt Vicki and that bottle.'

'You should both stay here,' Lance says, kissing me on my forehead. 'The weather's getting worse and you two are soaked to the skin. You should go and get changed into dry clothes.'

He's soaked too, but at least he's wearing a weatherproof jacket so part of his body is dry.

'What happened to the girls from the sanctuary?' I ask, realising I haven't seen them, or the animals, since returning to The Hall.

'They took the rest of the animals back to the sanctuary. Gwen went with them to help.' He grins suddenly. 'Hold on to your dress, Merrion, I'm opening the front door.'

'Oh ha bloody ha,' she says, but she grabs her hem and holds on to it for dear life. 'Bloody men,' she adds.

Ralph nudges her playfully before he and Reece, who has put a coat on over his saturated clothes, for some absurd reason, follow Lance out into what I can safely say is building up to be a very 'dark and stormy night'.

'Whisky?' Aunt Vicki pours herself a large glass and gingerly holds the bottle over an empty one.

'Absolutely.' Merrion marches over to the other winged chair and plonks herself down.

'Er. Yes please,' I say. 'But what just

happened, Merrion? Do you know that guy? You were acting rather strangely.'

'I was acting strangely! Did you see the way he grabbed me and dragged me in here?'

'He did seem a little... rough. But perhaps that's just his way.' I take the glass Aunt Vicki passes me and cradle it in my hands. 'And it was so windy out there, I'm sure he was simply trying to help.'

'Help? If that's his idea of help he needn't bother to help me ever again.' She empties her glass in two large gulps.

'Um. Am I missing something, Merrion?'

She ignores me and, taking the bottle from Aunt Vicki, pours herself another drink. I open my mouth to speak but Merrion glares at me.

'Don't say another word, Harri. I don't want to talk about it and you've said and done quite enough already.'

Aunt Vicki smiles and settles back into her chair, closing her eyes as she does so.

'Well Harriet dear,' she says. 'Today may not have been a complete waste of your time after all.'

I have absolutely no idea what she means by that so I swig my whisky and walk towards the window to peer out into the darkness. I hear a long, loud howl and it sends a shiver down my spine. I feel as if I'm in a scene from that Sherlock Holmes film: *The Hound of the Baskervilles*. Lance and I watched it on TV the other night and it scared the life out of me. The special effects were unbelievably realistic. I hope that scruffy Irish wolfhound hasn't just attacked Dan Barker. I know Lance and my family are safe because I can just make them out running towards the direction the howl came from.

'Do you think something's happened to the dog? Or perhaps it's attacked Dan Barker? It was pretty big.'

I turn and glance at Merrion who looks even more concerned than I am. She shifts in her seat then pours another drink and falls back against the padded leather.

'I hope the damn thing's eaten him.' She empties her glass and slams it down on the table. 'Come on, Aunt. I'll help you upstairs to bed.'

'I'm staying here, child. I want to see what's happened, and so do you, so stop behaving like a spoilt brat and go and get us some towels.'

Incredibly, Merrion does exactly as she's told.

We don't have long to wait. By the time Merrion's brought the towels, Lance pushes open one of the front doors and Ralph and Reece tumble into the Great Hall in front of him. Drowned rats would look dry in comparison to the three of them. They are literally dripping wet from head to toe.

'Where's Dan?' There's more than a hint of anxiety in Merrion's voice. 'I mean… did that dog have him for dinner?' She laughs, but it sounds weird.

'Dan's fine. And so is the dog.' Lance peels off his jacket and reaches out for one of the towels

Merrion is cradling. 'May I?'

'Oh, yes.' She hands him one and gives one each to Reece, Ralph, Aunt Vicki and finally, to me, leaving three in her arms. 'Where are they? I've got towels for them.'

'Who?' Lance drops his jacket on the floor and rubs his thick, black hair with the towel. 'Dan and the dog? They've gone. He wanted to get the dog back to the sanctuary and settled down as quickly as possible.'

'Well really,' she snaps. 'That's just bloody rude.' She throws the remaining towels on her empty chair and marches towards the stairs. 'I'm going to bed. And no, Harri, I don't want to talk about it. Good night.'

'Is it just me or is Merrion acting strangely tonight?'

None of the men say a word but Aunt Vicki chuckles quietly. I get the distinct impression she knows something I don't. But then Aunt Vicki always does.

Chapter Four

I love it when Lance stays the night and not just because of the sex, although that's great. Better than great. It's sensational! I know it's still relatively early days in our relationship but I have a feeling that sex between me and luscious Lance will always be sensational, even when we're ninety and everything creaks.

Now all that's creaking is my bed as I snuggle up against Lance, who has fallen back to sleep, and that's because it's well over ninety years old. It's an original Tudor oak bedstead and the one thing about it that's from this century is the mattress. That's brand new. But only because Lance bought it. He said if he was going to stay here on a regular basis (and if I had my way, he would never leave) he was damn well going to sleep on something he was sure wasn't made of straw, horse hair, and feathers from a bird that passed away several centuries earlier. He was exaggerating, of course. My mattress wasn't quite that old but it probably saw action during the First World War, if you know what I mean.

Needless to say, Lance knew someone who could get an unbelievably good deal on a job lot. He really does know a great many exceptionally handy people. So it wasn't just my bed that got a plush 5,000 pocket springs, British sheep, fleece wool padded, cotton-silk mix covered mattress. Lance got one for every member of my family and he wouldn't take a penny for any of them. For a builder, he seems to have a lot of spare cash lying around, but then he does own his own company.

Or perhaps his sister, Ophelia helps him out. Not only is she a chef of celebrity status, she's rich enough to have bought her own stately home and have her super-exclusive restaurant in the grounds. It's called *Ophelia's Garden* and Lance took me there on our first date – although it wasn't supposed to be a date because at the time I was still with Art, who was on his way over from Australia. But that's all irrelevant now.

Ophelia also owns a home in Aspen, Colorado. Which I've yet to visit. I've met her and she's lovely, just like his other sister, Gwen. They're both beautiful. They're both successful. And sometimes, they both make me feel like a bit of a loser. They don't mean to, of course. But Ophelia is a jet-setting business woman, wife and mother, with several cook books to her name as well as everything else and Gwen was... sorry, still is, married to one of the most famous English footballers of the last few years, Jackson Hunter. But Gwen says they hate each other's guts and she never wants to see him again unless it's to identify his corpse.

She apparently tried to kill him last year and got herself arrested for her efforts. I don't know the gory details and Lance told me it was nowhere near as bad as the media made out. She did get off, so I suppose he must be telling the truth and as Jackson dropped the charges, it can't have been too serious, in spite of what Merrion said yesterday in the car on the way home from hospital. I keep meaning to look it up on the internet but every time I start, I somehow feel guilty and delete my search. I really like Gwen and I'm not sure I want to read some highly fictitious and no doubt salacious version of the event. I'm hoping she will tell me the details herself one day.

Gwen followed in her sister's footsteps and started cooking, only she did it via the internet and, at the tender age of seventeen became an almost overnight sensation. She appeared on all sorts of TV shows, apparently and set up a company catering for celebrities' .parties. That's how she and Jackson met. Gwen was invited to cater for Jackson's twenty-fifth birthday party. Their eyes met across platters of baked mozzarella in pancetta and prawns with celeriac in champagne batter. Less than one month later, they were married.

Anyway, I'm not a loser, I know that. And I have Lance who loves me. That makes me the luckiest woman in the whole wide world. I haven't known him long, only since last December, and I've still got a lot to discover about him, but I've never felt like this about anyone and he says he feels the same about me. It's as if we were meant to be together. He told me he knew it the moment Ralph picked me up and threw me over his shoulder. He instantly felt protective of me and he only feels like that about his sisters and his dog. I wasn't quite sure how to take that when he said it but as he adores both his sisters and wouldn't be without Thunder, the stray dog he rescued and loves to bits, I know it meant I'm very special to him. I love everything about him. Every inch of his firm body, his raven black hair and dark brooding eyes, his gravelly voice and laugh, and the way his lips twitch when I say something I shouldn't. Which happens quite a lot. But I particularly love the way he smiles at me, even when he thinks I'm not looking. If only Merrion, Ralph and Gwen could be as happy as I am.

'Good morning, gorgeous.'

Lance is awake and looking at me and there's something bordering on salacious in his eyes. His sexy smile confirms it. He's thinking about sex and that's absolutely fine with me.

'Good morning, you sexy, insatiable hunk.'

That sounded better in my head but Lance grins and kisses me and all thoughts of Ophelia, Gwen and Jackson, and why anyone would think prawns with celeriac in champagne batter is a good recipe for a happy marriage, are gone from my mind in a flash. All I can think about now is that my new mattress and its 5,000 pocket springs are going to get another thorough testing.

Chapter Five

Merrion's already having breakfast when Lance and I enter the kitchen and I'm not sure what surprises me the most. That she's up at eight o'clock on a day when she doesn't have to work, or that she looks as if she's been awake all night.

Merrion usually sleeps like a log and she's one of those people who can fall asleep on a pinhead if that's the only place available. What's more, as she earns her living – and a very good living it is – as a model, her looks are important. She needs her beauty sleep. Although as she's mainly a lip model I suppose it's only her pouting, silky smooth mouth that has to look its best.

'Are you ill?' I ask, heading for the snazzy (and according to Merrion) incredibly expensive, *Jura* coffee machine, which Lance bought as a New Year present for our family.

'No.' She glances at me briefly before returning her gaze to her coffee mug.

'You look ill,' I persist. 'Doesn't she, Lance?'

He has a slightly worried look on his face and hesitates before he replies, as if he's not sure he wants to get caught in the middle of something.

'Um. I've seen you looking better, Merrion. That much is true.'

He bends down to stroke his dog, Thunder, who is curled up in his basket fast asleep. This is also somewhat surprising. The mad little thing is usually bouncing around like a jumping-jack the second he hears Lance's voice. Thankfully, he wakes up the moment Lance touches him, and immediately starts bouncing and barking. At least he's okay. That's one less thing to worry about.

Merrion smiles at Thunder and at Lance. 'I took him out for a long walk earlier. I couldn't sleep.'

'Why not?' I ask, grabbing the bread from the breadbin. 'I thought you'd be as shattered as I was. What's wrong?'

'I'm worried about Mum, that's all.'

'Oh why? What's happened? Has Dad called? Did he come home?' I look around me as if I half expect Dad to suddenly appear.

'No one's called and everything's fine, I'm sure. But I don't think he came home last night and I can't help worrying. Okay? She's my mum and she's not a youngster.' Merrion lets out a long and soulful sigh before throwing me a tiny smile. 'Sorry. I'm tired and ratty. Ignore me.'

I discard the bread and go to her, wrapping my arm around her shoulder.

'Of course you're worried. We all are. But Bella's fit and strong and… well, it's not her first time, is it? She's done it four times already. Five if you count the twins as two births. And let's face it, those two were probably a nightmare.' I laugh and Merrion's smile grows.

'I don't know. I seem to recall they were born and screaming their little lungs out before we made it to the hospital.'

That's true. And they were born a few weeks early. We all joked afterwards that they couldn't wait to get out and see what mischief they could make.

'Perhaps this baby will come early too. I'm sure it'll go without a hitch.'

Aunt Vicki pushes the kitchen door open. 'What will go without a hitch? Those were the very words you used about yesterday's tea party. I think we can all agree that you were wrong. I hope you're not concocting another ridiculous plan to find the perfect partners for your step-siblings, because frankly, child, I don't think my nerves could take it. Lance? Are you making coffee? Put a dash of whisky in mine, would you?'

Lance grins at her and makes the coffee but he gives me a sideways glance and there's a question in his eyes. I hadn't told him my plan. But then I hadn't told anyone and everyone seems to be aware of it. Well, at least Merrion and Aunt Vicki do.

'I don't know what you mean, Aunt. I was

hoping some abandoned animals might get a new home, that's all. And that the Hall's Cross Animal Rescue Sanctuary would get some much needed, additional funds.'

Aunt Vicki shakes her head and smiles. 'Of course you were, my dear. Instead, it seems the sanctuary got a new manager. He was quite good looking, don't you think, Merrion?'

Merrion looks startled. 'What? No I don't. I didn't notice. I only saw him for a few minutes. I wasn't at all impressed. He smelt of dog.'

'He didn't smell of dog, Merrion,' Lance says. 'He may have done by the time he returned to the sanctuary but when he arrived he smelt of aftershave, and he hadn't been here long, so I'm sure it hadn't worn off when he helped you inside.'

I must be giving him an odd look because he bursts out laughing.

'He overdid it,' Lance continues. 'With the aftershave. He mentioned it almost as soon as he got out of his car. He apologised and said that he was getting ready to go out on a date when he received the call about the *Great Escape*. In his haste, he forgot he had the bottle in his hand, and threw it all over himself.'

'A date?' Merrion glares at Lance. 'With whom?'

'I didn't ask and he didn't say. I was surprised he said as much as he did. But he did smell like a Paris brothel so I suppose he felt he had to explain. Not that I know what a Paris brothel smells like before any of you pick up on that. Does it matter who his date was with?'

'No. No it doesn't matter one bit. I couldn't care less who the man goes out with. I hope he drowns himself in aftershave.'

She jumps up from her chair and storms out, leaving the kitchen door swinging wildly in her wake.

'What just happened?' I ask. 'Merrion really is behaving strangely. Why is she so angry with a man she hadn't met until last night? I don't get it.'

'Which is why, Harriet dear, you'll never be a matchmaker,' Aunt Vicki says. 'Lance. Are those beans still on the way from Brazil or might I expect a cup of coffee sometime in the near future?'

Chapter Six

Bella is coming home either later today or tomorrow, Dad calls to inform us at a little after eight-thirty. And so is Lucinda Victoria Hall, the newest addition to the extended Hamilton-Hall family who arrived shortly before midnight, much to everyone's surprise and with hardly any warning. The seven pound eight ounce bundle of joy is fit and healthy, and so is Bella.

'Oh Dad, that's wonderful,' I say, bursting into tears with a mixture of relief and joy. 'Let me put you on speaker so that Aunt Vicki and Lance can hear you.'

Dad repeats what he's just told me and now Aunt Vicki's crying too.

'You have named her Victoria after me, Wyndham? That's so kind of you, my boy. And Lucinda is in honour of your dear, departed mother, of course.' She removes the whitest, mostly crisply-starched cotton handkerchief I have ever seen from the sleeve of the black cardigan she's wearing, and blows her nose rather loudly.

I don't think I've ever seen Aunt Vicki cry like this. Not with happiness. I've only seen her shed tears of sorrow, twice. Once when my mum died and the second time, when I left for Australia, now that I think about it. I stare at her for a second whilst she asks Dad if baby Lucinda Victoria looks anything like her. I sincerely hope not, but then I remember seeing photographs of her when she was young, and she was very pretty so perhaps it isn't so bad. Then I realise that I must go and find the others and tell them the exciting news.

'I'll go,' says Lance, apparently reading my mind. I don't know how he does it but sometimes he seems to know exactly what I'm thinking. 'Congratulations, Wyndham,' he adds, as he heads towards the door.

'Thank you, Lance,' Dad replies, his voice cracking with emotion after his chat with Aunt Vicki.

Lance hurries into the Great Hall with Thunder at his heels, and shouts for everyone to come immediately to the kitchen. Clearly they all hear him. A herd of stampeding elephants would make less noise than my relatives who come thundering down the stairs and burst into the room, eyes aglow and chests heaving from the sudden exertion.

'What's happened?' Merrion breathlessly demands. 'Is it Mum?'

Dad repeats his news for a third time and then

he can't be heard over the shrieks of delight and thuds on the floor as we all jump up and down and hug one another. The twins come bounding in and join us, although it's clear they have no idea why we're all so excited. Aunt Vicki calls them to her and whispers in their ears. Then no one can be heard above their deafening screams and Thunder's excited bark.

I take the phone off speaker. 'I think you can tell we're all over the moon, Dad.'

He laughs on the other end of the line. 'Is that what it is? For a moment I thought some wild animals had got loose in The Hall.'

'No animals of any kind, here, Dad. They're all safely back in their cosy little living quarters at the sanctuary. Unless you count the twins. Oh, and Thunder. But he's not wild, merely crazy. Give Bella all our love. When can we come and see her and baby Lucinda?'

'Later today. They're both fast asleep right now. Visiting starts at two but there may be some flexibility. Having said that, we may be coming home today. You know what these hospitals are like these days. They want you out at the soonest opportunity. I'll call you in a couple of hours or so to provide you with an update.'

'Thanks, Dad. We'll wait to hear from you. And Dad…'

'Yes, sweetheart.'

'I am so, so sorry about what happened yesterday.'

'Why? What happened yesterday? The only thing I can recall is my darling wife giving me a gorgeous baby daughter named Lucinda Victoria Hall.'

I swallow a lump in my throat. Dad has clearly forgiven me. Then, for the tiniest, briefest, shortest moment, I feel an utterly stupid pang of jealousy. It's crazy I know, but until last night, I was his only biological daughter. I had a similar feeling for a nanosecond when the twins were born except with them it was slightly different. Dad had always wanted a son but after I was born and Mum got cancer, there wasn't much chance of that happening. That's one of the reasons I shortened my name from Harriet to Harri. It sounds ridiculous now, but I wanted to be everything to Dad. Both his daughter and his son. When he and Bella married almost fifteen years ago, he got Ralph and Reece and also Merrion but I was still his only blood-child. And then, almost four and a half years ago, the twins came along. Don't get me wrong, I love them to the ends of the earth despite what I say about them. But they were the sons he'd always craved. It didn't change the way he felt about me and I know what he feels for Lucinda won't alter that either. I'm being an idiot.

'And Harri…,' he continues, his voice full of love.

'Yes, Dad.'

'I can't wait for my other gorgeous daughter to meet her. And for my wonderful stepchildren to meet her too.'

I wipe the tears from my eyes and try to catch my breath. 'I love you, Dad.'

'I love you too, sweetheart. And I always will, no matter what. I love you all.'

Chapter Seven

No matter how much I scrub the oak floor of the Great Hall, I can't seem to get rid of the smell, or the stains, from the dog pee and poo. I'll be here until Christmas at this rate even with Merrion's help.

'Try this, Hairy,' Reece says.

I wish he would stop calling me that. Unfortunately, he couldn't pronounce Harriet when he was young and instead of Harri, he mistakenly pronounced it as 'Hairy'. It was amusing at the time but it kind of stuck and to him, I suppose I'll always be 'Hairy'. He's holding a glass bottle, full of bubbling liquid which frankly, I don't like the look of.

'What it is?'

'It's a cleaning liquid I've invented. I believe I can categorically state that it will remove all trace of unpleasant odours and unsightly stains.'

'It'll probably burn a hole in the floor,' Merrion says, giving Reece a look of distrust.

Reece pushes his glasses back in place. 'I can assure you it won't. I have tested it thoroughly.'

'Hmm.' I take the bottle from him and almost gag. 'Good grief, Reece. It smells worse than the dog piddle.'

'That is temporary. The smell will disappear as the chemicals evaporate. Oh. But it would be wise to wear two pairs of rubber gloves. To quote Aunt Vicki: "It's better to be safe than sorry," and there is a slight possibility that if it comes into contact with your skin, you may suffer with a rash. Or mild burns.'

'Reece!' Merrion gets to her feet and thumps him on the arm.

'Ow. What was that for? I'm trying to be of help.'

'By giving us third degree burns?'

'Not if you wear gloves. It works, Merrion. Trust me.' He looks a little put out by her lack of gratitude.

'You want to help?' Merrion removes her gloves and slaps them against his chest. 'Then you wear the gloves and you get down on the floor and use your concoction to clean it.'

'Certainly. If that would help.'

To my amazement, not only does Reece do as Merrion instructs, but his cleaning liquid actually works. The horrid smells of the chemicals, together with the pungent odour of dog deposits, waft away within minutes and the floor looks almost as good as it did the day before my disastrous afternoon tea party.

'Wow, Reece. It works.'

He glances up at me and his glasses slide down the length of his nose. 'I know it does. I told you it would.'

'Reece?' Aunt Vicki appears at the sitting room door. 'I sincerely hope that isn't my cocktail you are using to clean the floor.'

'No, Aunt. It isn't.'

'What a relief. If that is what it does to the floor, just think what it would do to my internal organs.'

'Nothing more than all the years of drinking alcohol has done,' Merrion whispers to me.

Aunt Vicki glowers at her. 'I'm not deaf, young lady.'

Merrion grins and adeptly changes the subject. 'Tell us about the balls held here when you were my age, Aunt.'

Aunt Vicki seems surprised. A wistful look appears in her eyes as she walks towards one of the winged chairs and sits back against the cushion. 'Those were the days when young people knew how to dance. Not all this jiggery-pokery you call dancing. We waltzed. We drank champagne. We fell in love. We strolled in the moonlight and stole secret kisses beneath starlit skies. Ooh, if only I could turn back the clock and relive that time once more.' A long, slow sigh escapes her. 'But why did you ask that?'

Merrion shrugs. 'No reason.'

'Harriet? This doesn't have anything to do with some new hair-brained scheme of yours, does it?'

'What?' Now I'm the one who's surprised. 'No, Aunt.'

Her eyes narrow as if she doesn't quite believe me even though I'm telling the truth. I haven't a clue why Merrion brought up the balls from the old days.

But it has given me an idea. An absolutely wonderful idea. And I can't wait to get to my iPad and start searching the internet to see exactly what I'll need to do.

Chapter Eight

'You want to do what?' Dad's ginger-grey brows furrow and his hands clasp in an almost prayer-like fashion as he rests them on his desk and slumps back in the leather chair in his study.

He doesn't seem as pleased as I'd hoped, but that may be because he's over tired. He was up all night when Bella gave birth and he didn't get any rest when they brought little Lucinda home late yesterday afternoon. Every one of us was fussing and cooing over Dad, Bella and the baby. He didn't get much sleep last night either, if the screams I heard for most of it were anything to go by. Lucinda may be cute but my God, that kid's got a pair of lungs on her. She's clearly not happy to have arrived in this world four weeks earlier than scheduled and she's determined to let all of us know it. Bella's equally as shattered as Dad. Merrion, Aunt Vicki and I have been helping out as much as possible since they came home. But changing nappies is as awful as I remembered it to be when I helped out with the twins.

Today, several of the villagers arrived with flowers and gifts for Bella and the little one, so Dad hasn't been able to grab forty winks so far, either. He had to be friendly and polite, in spite of looking as if he might keel over at any moment. Personally, I thought it was a bit rude of them to call so soon, but as they all said they had been extremely anxious for poor dear Bella after the 'incident' at the tea party, we couldn't simply take the gifts and tell them to come back later to see the baby, could we?

I smile at Dad and persevere. 'I want to organise a ball, partly to welcome Lucinda into the world and partly because Aunt Vicki is ninety in June and we really ought to do something special to mark the occasion. We'll call it The Starlight Ball because Aunt Vicki made dancing under the stars sound so romantic.'

'Victoria made it sound romantic? Our Victoria?'

'Yes.'

'Well, I'll be damned.' He rubs his chin with his thumb and forefinger. 'I suppose there is romance in all of us.'

'I mentioned it to Bella earlier and she liked the idea, but she was rather tired so I'm not sure it really sunk in. And this time I'd organise it properly. I'd get professionals in to help and we'll have an orchestra, a catering company to provide the food and drink together with waiting staff.

Maybe even a party planner to do the decorations.'

'Decorations? What sort of decorations?'

'Oh you know, just lights, bunting and stuff. Oh, and we'd have to have a cake. Two cakes, in fact. One for Aunt Vicki and one for Lucinda.'

'It sounds expensive. I will admit that we should celebrate both Lucinda's arrival and Victoria's ninetieth, but do we have to have something on such a grand scale? Couldn't we merely have a special dinner? Or possibly a cocktail party? I don't think we can afford a ball.' He shakes his head and his eyelids flicker as a yawn escapes him.

'That's the beauty of it, Dad. It needn't cost us a penny.'

'Please don't tell me you've persuaded Lance to pay for it.'

'Er. I haven't mentioned it to Lance yet. I only thought of it yesterday after something Aunt Vicki said and I wanted to research the possibility thoroughly and check with Bella and you before I mentioned it to him or anyone else. No point in getting anyone's hopes up if you and Bella were against it.'

'I don't think we would be against it, exactly, sweetheart, but it does sound as if there would be an awful lot of preparation involved and it's only a matter of weeks away. Is it feasible to put such a shindig together in such a short space of time? And if so, why wouldn't it cost us a penny? I'm not sure I follow this at all. How could we hold a ball for free?'

'We make it a charity event and charge for the tickets. All the profits would go to the charity after we'd covered our costs.'

'I'm not sure that's quite fair, sweetheart. We would be getting other people to pay for Victoria and Lucinda's party. Is that ethical?'

'People pay to go to dinner dances all the time. That's what they'd be doing here. But they'd also get a personal invitation to attend the celebration of Lucinda Victoria Hall's birth and Victoria Elizabeth Margaret Fitzroy Hall's ninetieth birthday. We'd have flashy invitations made that people could keep. Lots of them would love to stick that on their display shelves or mantelpieces.'

'Would they? How odd. It's not an invitation from the Queen.'

'No. But it is an invitation from The Halls of The Hall and if it's gold edged and embossed, they'll think it's wonderful, believe me, Dad.'

'I'm sure you know more about these things than I, so I'll defer to your knowledge. Do you have a particular charity in mind?'

'Um. I was thinking of the Hall's Cross Animal Rescue Sanctuary. That would make up for the fact that the tea party didn't go quite as well as I'd hoped.'

To my complete surprise, Dad bursts out laughing, but a few moments later, he's deadly serious.

'There won't be animals involved, will there?

You're not planning a repeat performance.'

'Absolutely not, Dad. There won't be an animal in site. Not one, I promise. I'll even tell Lance he'll have to leave Thunder at home.'

'Oh, I believe we can make an exception for Thunder.' He gives me a tiny smile and winks. 'I assume you want it to be as much of a surprise for Victoria as possible. Are you going to pretend it's merely Lucinda's arrival we are celebrating?'

'Something like that, yes.'

He nods and I can see that he's inclined to give me the go-ahead.

'Let me speak to Bella about it, sweetheart, and we'll talk again later. I think it's a marvellous idea in many ways. And Victoria certainly did love those balls. I remember her speaking endlessly about them when I was younger. Perhaps we can persuade some of Victoria's old set to attend. It would be a walk down memory lane for them.'

'Are any of them still alive? She doesn't see many of her old friends as far as I know.'

He shrugs and shakes his head. 'Bella would know. She helps Victoria write her Christmas cards.'

'Brilliant! I'd better get things moving then. As you said, it's only a matter of weeks and there's so much to do.'

I dash to his side, kiss him on the cheek and race towards the door.

'But I haven't discussed it with Bella yet,' he calls after me.

I blow him a kiss and give a little wave as I close the door behind me. I know I don't have a thing to worry about on that score. Bella will say yes. I'm more concerned about the Hall's Cross Animal Rescue Sanctuary. I'm not sure Daniel Barker will be so easily won over. If only Merrion hadn't taken such an instant dislike to him. With nothing more than a smile, she can usually persuade any man to do anything she wants them to. But possibly not Daniel Barker.

Chapter Nine

'You want to do what?'

Why does everyone keep asking me that question? Bella said exactly the same thing when I mentioned my idea to her, as did Dad. And now Lance. Why doesn't anyone say: 'Wow, Harriet, I think that's a brilliant idea. How can I help?' Or words to that effect. Why do they all look and sound as if they think I'm mad?

'I want to organise a charity ball,' I repeat.

Lance stares at me in disbelief as he opens the door so I walk ahead of him and, grabbing a bottle of wine from the rack, pour myself a glass even though I'm in his kitchen and he hasn't offered me one.

'Help yourself,' he says, taking off his work jacket and hanging it in the hall closet. But he says it with a smile so I know he doesn't mind in the least that I consider his place my second home.

'Would you like one?' I shake the bottle to and fro.

'How kind,' he quips. 'I'd like a large one, but I've got to pick Gwen up so I'd better wait until later. Are you staying, or did you just pop round to share your exciting news?'

He kicks off his steel-toe-capped boots and saunters towards me with a look in his dark eyes that I've come to know so well since Christmas. I'm rather glad I decided to nip down and wait for him to get home from work.

We hadn't planned to see one another this evening because tonight he's going to the local pub, The Cross in Hand, with my stepbrother, Ralph and some friends from the Hall's Cross Rugby Club.

I'm going to be cooking dinner for my family this evening and, as I tend to make rather a lot of mess whenever I cook, I'll be spending most of my night cleaning the kitchen.

He pulls me into his arms and I smile up at him. 'Just came to share my news. But I'm more than happy to stay for half an hour or so. What did you have in mind?'

His smile is decidedly wicked. 'How about a game of strip poker? But without the cards.' He kisses me and I immediately start tugging at his shirt.

'Oh wait! Where's Gwen?' I ask, somewhat breathlessly because judging by the speed at which he's unbuttoning my blouse, it's clear we won't be moving from the kitchen.

'Do you ever listen to me?' he whispers into

my ear. 'I told you I've got to collect her from the animal sanctuary in an hour.' His mouth glides downwards to my neck.

I don't recall him saying that, but it doesn't matter. It means she won't burst in on us and that's what's important. We almost got caught *in flagrante* once before, and I would rather not repeat that performance.

'Plenty of time then.' A thought pops into my head. 'Why's Gwen at the animal sanctuary?'

He stops what he's doing and looks into my eyes. 'You want to discuss Gwen's activities now?' A sexy smile hovers on his lips and he traces one finger across mine. 'Are you sure?'

I lick it with the tip of my tongue and shake my head very, very slowly. 'No. But I would like to discuss it later. I need a word with Daniel Barker and if Gwen's getting on friendly terms with him, it would help me no end.'

'Fine. We'll discuss it later. Much, much later. Now can we please get back to what we were doing?'

'Carry on, sir,' I say.

He does. And Gwen, Daniel, The Starlight Ball and even my family are rapidly forgotten.

Chapter Ten

Lance is late to collect Gwen but when we pull up in the virtually empty car park of the Hall's Cross Animal Rescue Sanctuary, she's standing outside with Daniel Barker and they're both laughing hysterically. They're looking up at the white and green signage; other than it being caked in grime and the letters 'i' and 'm' in 'Animal' being missing, I can't see what's so amusing about it.

'What's so funny?' I ask, getting out of my car and waiting for Lance to get out of his. He'd suggested that if I wanted to have a word with Daniel about my idea, now would be as good a time as any.

Gwen turns to look at me and I can't recall ever having seen her so happy. I wonder if Daniel Barker is married. Or has a girlfriend. Then I remember Lance saying that Daniel was getting ready to go out on a date on the day of the disastrous tea party, so I suppose he must have. Unless it was a first date. I must find out, but more importantly, I need to get him to see why The Starlight Ball would be both the perfect way for me and my family to apologise, and also to get those much needed funds for the sanctuary.

'Can't you see it?' Gwen asks, pointing up at the sign.

'If you want that fixed,' Lance says, grinning, 'I know a man who does signage at extremely competitive prices.'

I study it and tilt my head from side to side and finally, I see what's making them laugh. The word 'Animal' now reads as 'An..al'.

'I don't know,' Daniel replies. 'I'm thinking of leaving it. There are a lot of arses around here that may need rescuing. Including mine, after that delightful afternoon your girlfriend so kindly arranged.'

'It wasn't my fault the animals escaped.'

I didn't mean to shriek quite so loud but for heaven's sake, why can't anyone see I meant well?

Daniel raises blond eyebrows and I notice he grins at Lance. 'Don't worry,' he says. 'I know you had the best intentions. No one was hurt and no animals were physically harmed. I wasn't sure as to their mental state after their exciting day out, but they all seem fine to me.'

'Why did you come in two cars?' Gwen asks, walking towards me and kissing me on the cheek before doing the same to Lance.

'Oh,' I say, glancing down at the cracked tarmac and pressing a loose chunk back into place with my shoe. 'Um. Now may not be a good time, but I wanted to have a quick word with Mr Barker. Then I'm off home to cook dinner for the family.'

'Call me Dan,' Daniel says. 'And now is fine. What's it about? Are you considering adopting an animal?'

'No way.' I realise I said that a little too quickly and emphatically, so I hastily add: 'Lance brings Thunder to The Hall all the time, so in a way, I feel as if I already have a dog. He's there today, in fact. I sometimes have him when Lance is at work and when Gwen or the Tarrants who often look after him, are busy. And he's a rescue dog. Lance rescued him. It was during a thunder storm. That's why Gwen suggested calling him, Thunder.' And now I'm babbling like a lunatic.

Daniel seems to be having trouble with his lip, because he's been biting it throughout my little speech.

'That's good.' He glances at Gwen and Lance.

'Harriet gets a tiny bit carried away at times,' Lance informs him with a little laugh. 'But I love her, and you will too. Only not too much, I hope.'

'I do not,' I say, somewhat peevishly. 'Well okay, perhaps just the teensiest bit. But it's important to explain things.'

'Of course it is my darling.' Lance comes to me and wraps his arms around me. 'And now I'm going to take Gwen home, and leave you here to explain your latest idea to Dan.'

'Ooh! What idea?' Gwen asks.

Lance closes his eyes for one second then glances over his shoulder at his sister. 'I should have known that was a mistake.' He kisses me on the lips and takes my hand in his. 'Come on then, Harriet. Tell Gwen and Dan all about your latest and greatest plan. But don't forget I'm meeting Ralph in an hour and I still need to take a shower.'

Chapter Eleven

I'm very pleased that Gwen loved my idea immediately and was so excited that she offered to help in any way she could. She even suggested that she could do the catering, which was a complete surprise. Since her break-up with Jackson Hunter and her brush with the law, she hasn't catered any functions, apparently. She's hardly done any cooking for that matter, so I'm told. At first, Lance seemed as stunned by her offer as I was, but then he looked pleased, so I instantly agreed. I can't wait to see what she has in mind.

Dan took a little longer to convince but he warmed to my plan eventually and Lance was probably only half an hour or so late to meet Ralph in the pub. Once I'd explained in detail what it would involve and shown Dan some photos and drawings on my iPad, which thankfully I'd taken with me to Lance's, he said that he could see it had possibilities. He wasn't sure about having photos of the animals made into bunting though, especially as we were supposed to be celebrating the arrival of Lucinda. And Aunt Vicki's ninetieth birthday.

'Pictures of dogs, cats and various other animals may seem slightly out of place for such an event, don't you think?' he asked. 'Even if they are attached to brightly coloured ribbons and strung around the Great Hall of The Hall.'

'Oh I'll have some made with photos of Aunt Vicki and some of Lucinda too, so it won't just be the animals,' I assured him. 'We've already taken hundreds of photos of my baby sister. I'm sure there must be some where she doesn't look as if her head is made of beetroot and she's not screaming her lungs out. And there's bound to be tons of photos of Aunt Vicki in one of the boxes in the attic. I know there're only a few in various rooms in the house but I'll find the rest. It'll be fine. Don't worry about a thing.'

Lance had merely chuckled whilst Gwen had made a couple of sensible, alternative suggestions.

'Why don't we have balloons made with photos of Lucinda on them? And what about getting some cheap but elegant champagne flutes and having Aunt Vicki's and Lucinda's names, together with their dates of birth, etched on the base of each. That way the glasses would be additional keepsakes for those attending the ball.'

'That's a brilliant idea,' I said. 'That would also mean we don't have to do so much washing up. The guests can wash their own glasses when they get them home.'

I still find it a little odd that Gwen calls Aunt Vicki, Aunt Vicki, if you see what I mean. Lance just calls her Vicki, but Gwen says she couldn't possibly do that, so Aunt Vicki it is, and Aunt Vicki doesn't seem to mind. My great aunt really has mellowed since I left for Australia.

Gwen's idea was definitely an excellent one. Especially bearing in mind that Aunt Vicki might not take kindly to having her likeness on display. For some reason, she dislikes seeing photos of herself. That's why there aren't many in the house. The moment someone puts a picture of her in a frame, it suddenly disappears from view. Aunt Vicki says it's ghosts, but we all know she's got them stashed somewhere, either in her room or in the attic.

Lance had added: 'I think I know someone who may be able to get us some top quality crystal flutes at rock-bottom prices. Leave that with me. I'll be seeing him tonight in the pub.'

So we left it on that note and I headed home to cook dinner whilst Lance and Gwen headed back to his place. Dan, it seemed, was off out on another date. Well, the same date really; the one he had had to cancel because of the escaped animals. Which was a pity because he and Gwen certainly seemed to be hitting it off. I suppose he may be a bit too old for Gwen though. She's still only eighteen after all, so a twenty-eight-year old man – even one who is the complete opposite of her ex-husband, Jackson Hunter – is probably not the perfect partner for her.

I do wish Merrion had been with me. I think she might have changed her opinion of Dan if she'd been there today. And as Merrion's almost twenty-six, they're the perfect age for one another. They have the same colour hair too and Dan's eyes are blue although not quite the same bright blue as Merrion's.

Attraction's such a funny thing. Under normal circumstances I would have bet my final pound that Dan was exactly the type of man that Merrion would get the hots for. Oh well, it seems I can be wrong on occasion. It was abundantly clear that Merrion didn't like Daniel Barker. Not one tiny little bit. There wasn't as much as the minutest spark of chemistry between them. But then it had been pouring with rain and blowing a gale and he did virtually drag her up the steps to The Hall. Perhaps if they had met in better circumstances it might have been an entirely different story.

Chapter Twelve

'Are you completely mad?'

Merrion glares at me over her morning coffee and Ralph emits a little cough before hiding his face behind a newspaper.

'Why? What have I done now?'

'It's not what you've done, it's what you're planning to do.'

I amble over to the coffee machine and pour myself a large coffee. I didn't get much sleep last night. I kept going over my plans in my head and before I knew it, it was eight o'clock in the morning and time to get up. Not that I really have to get up at any particular time. It's not as if I have a job to go to or anything. I suppose I should do something about that situation before much longer, but Lance said that I should enjoy some free time with my family after having been away from them for two years... so I am. Besides, now that little Lucinda's arrived, Bella could probably use all the help she can get around here.

On my way back to the kitchen table, I give Ralph a gentle slap on the back of his head. 'I suppose this means that Lance told you all about The Starlight Ball in the pub last night, Ralph, and this morning you told Merrion. I hope you haven't told Aunt Vicki because it's supposed to be a surprise.'

'Oh it'll be a surprise all right,' Merrion says.

'I didn't know it was meant to be a secret.' Ralph frowns at me and smoothes his blond hair back into place.

'When, exactly, were you planning on telling me about this?' Merrion doesn't look happy.

'You're becoming a bit of a grouch lately,' I tell her. 'And I was going to talk to you, Ralph and Reece about it this morning, actually. I merely wanted to check with Dan before saying anything.'

Dan? Oh my God. Not... that dreadful man from the animal place. What's he got to do with it?'

Ralph tuts. 'I told you, silly. It's a charity ball.'

'I know you told me that. But you omitted to mention the charity. I assumed, seeing as this is supposed to be in celebration of Lucinda's birth and Aunt Vicki's ninetieth, that it would be a children or baby charity and possibly the Alzheimer's Society or Help the Aged or something.'

'Oh.' I pull out a chair and sit. 'I hadn't thought of that. But it's too late now. I've already told Dan and he's agreed.'

'Agreed to what?' Merrion's knuckles turn white as she grips her coffee cup.

'Agreed that it will be in aid of The Hall's Cross Animal Rescue Sanctuary. Or The Hall's Cross Anal Rescue Sanctuary, as it's currently called.' I grin but Ralph and Merrion exchange confused looks, so I have to explain. Ralph laughs but Merrion seems crosser than she already was.

'The only arse in Hall's Cross is Daniel bloody Barker.' She thumps her cup down on the table and the sound of scraping chair legs on the tiled floor sets my teeth on edge.

'Where are you going? Don't you want to hear about The Starlight Ball?'

'No I bloody well don't.'

The kitchen door bangs to and fro as she storms out into the Great Hall.

'What's up with her?' I ask an equally bewildered, Ralph.

He shrugs and folds up the newspaper. 'Don't ask me. She's hardly spoken a civil word to me in days.'

Bella appears, grabs the swinging door and glances back over her shoulder. 'Good gracious. What's the matter with Merrion this morning? She very nearly knocked me over in her haste and merely grunted when I wished her good morning. Thank goodness I wasn't carrying little Lucinda who is still upstairs with her father.'

'She's been in a bad mood since the tea party,' Ralph says. 'Would you like some coffee, Mum?

I'm getting myself another cup.'

'I would give anything for a cup of coffee, my darling. Thank you.' Bella comes and sits beside me, giving me a hug and kissing me on the cheek. 'And how are you this morning, dearest? Your father tells me you're definitely going ahead with your plans for The Starlight Ball.'

'I am. If you're absolutely certain you're happy for me to proceed. It's not too soon after the birth or anything, is it?'

Bella shakes her head and smiles. 'It's the 24th of June, isn't it?' I nod and she continues: 'That's four weeks away. I'll be feeling much more like dancing by then, sweetheart. And hopefully we'll all have had lots of sleep during the course of those four weeks too. Lucinda was so much more peaceful last night, don't you think?'

'Definitely.'

Ralph brings the coffee and hands it to Bella. 'I only heard her once, but then I didn't get home until about one-thirty.'

'Did you go back to Lance's?' I ask.

'No. I stayed on at the pub.'

'Doesn't The Cross in Hand close at eleven on a week night?' Bella takes a sip of coffee and closes her eyes as if she's drinking the nectar of the gods.

'Yes,' says Ralph, grinning. 'But Jodie lives upstairs.'

'Jodie? The barmaid? So you've finally asked her out.' I can't quite believe it. He's fancied her for ages apparently but he denied it for months before I came home and he's denied it every time I've asked him.

His grin widens. 'I didn't ask her out, exactly. We stayed in.'

'Yes. Thank you darling.' Bella shifts in her seat. 'I don't think we need the details before we've eaten breakfast. Does this mean you're a couple now?'

He frowns slightly. 'I don't know about that, Mum. She's only recently finished with her long-term boyfriend and I think he ended things with her, so I'm not entirely convinced she's over it. I don't want to rush into anything.'

'Rush into anything!' I repeat. 'You've been after her for months. You simply refused to admit it.'

He shrugs and drinks his coffee whilst Bella and I exchange glances.

'That's it? That's all you've got to say on the subject?' I shouldn't push him for an answer but I can't leave it at that.

'What do you want me to say? That I heard violins and got shot in the arse with cupid's arrow?'

'Language, darling.'

'Sorry, Mum. Oh. Did Harri tell you about the signage at the Hall's Cross Animal Rescue Sanctuary?'

'Yes darling, she did. And I think the sooner Lance gets his man to sort that out, the better.'

'Don't change the subject, Ralph.' I pinch his arm. 'Tell me how you feel about Jodie. Do you love her?'

He blinks several times and rubs the red mark on his skin. 'I like her and I find her attractive. Can we leave it at that, please? And don't start planning any engagement parties any time soon. Okay?'

'Okay. Okay. What is wrong with everyone lately?'

'Lack of sleep, I should imagine.' Aunt Vicki ambles into the kitchen and drops onto a chair. 'Get me some coffee, please, Ralph. There's a dear. Tell me, Bella, my sweet. Have you and Wyndham considered investing in a dummy for that child of yours? She's loud enough to wake the dead.'

'Babies tend to make a good deal of noise, Vicki. I'm sorry but that's the way it is. We're hoping she'll settle soon. She only cried once last night.'

'Cried? Screamed blue murder I think you mean. I sometimes thank my lucky stars I didn't have a child of my own. If he or she had been anything like Theo and Thor and now dear little Lucinda, I doubt they would have lived to see maturity.'

'Aunt Vicki! That's not very nice.'

She narrows her eyes at me. 'I'm nearly ninety, child. I don't need to be nice at my age.'

'Has Reece put something in the water?' I ask. 'Everyone around here is snapping like a river full of crocodiles. We should all be happy. We've got so much to look forward to. And Lucinda may be loud but she's a tiny, beautiful baby.'

'I didn't say she wasn't beautiful. I simply wish she wouldn't make her presence quite so well-known at three o'clock in the morning, that's all.'

Bella pats my hand. 'I expect it's merely because there has been rather a lot going on of late, sweetheart. We'll all be fine in a couple of days, I'm sure. And think what fun we'll all have organising this ball of yours.'

Too late, I try to stop Bella from saying those words.

'Ball?' Aunt Vicki sits upright. 'What ball? Is this another of your hair-brained schemes, Harriet?'

'Nothing's decided,' I lie. 'We're considering having a ball to welcome Lucinda into the world and it'll be in aid of charity. The Hall's Cross Animal Rescue Sanctuary to be precise.'

'The Hall's Cross... dear God, child. Haven't you done quite enough for that already? And why are you having a ball for Lucinda? She will hardly be able to appreciate it.'

'It's a ball because we're going to charge people for the tickets. That way I can make up for what happened at the tea party. I don't think many people remembered to donate after all the... excitement started. Plus, the ball will be a celebration of Lucinda's arrival.'

'I think it's a wonderful idea,' Bella says,

smiling apologetically at me.

Aunt Vicki glances from Bella to Ralph and finally to me. 'I suppose we should do something to formally announce little Lucinda as part of the Hall family. I'm not convinced a ball is quite the thing but if you're happy with the proposal, Bella and I assume Wyndham agrees, then who am I to stop you. I know everything there is to know about organising a ball, Harriet, so if you feel the event might benefit from my assistance, you know you only have to ask. Now is someone going to make some breakfast or am I going to starve to death a mere few weeks before my ninetieth birthday?'

Chapter Thirteen

I'm still hoping we got away with it this morning. The very fact Aunt Vicki felt she needed to remind us of her upcoming ninetieth, seemed to indicate she believes The Starlight Ball is only to celebrate Lucinda's arrival and has nothing to do with her own birthday which is good. It also means I can, as she very kindly suggested, benefit from her years of knowledge and experience. And that's no bad thing because frankly, as much as I hate to admit it, the longer my list of 'things to do' becomes, the more I begin to realise I have no idea how to organise a ball, and with only four weeks to go, there is very little time. I think I'm going to need all the help I can get.

And something else occurred to me during breakfast. I don't possess a ball gown.

Aunt Vicki was reminiscing about the old days and when she mentioned the beautiful gowns she used to wear, some of which she is sure are packed away in boxes in the attic, I realised I was going to have to get one. This may be a bit of a problem because my savings are running low. But I have no intention of borrowing one of Aunt Vicki's, however gorgeous they may be, so something needs to be done. Clearly I didn't think this through. I sometimes wish I could learn to take things slowly and not rush headlong into something simply because it seems like a good idea.

I wonder if Lance knows someone who can get me an exceptionally good deal on a Vera Wang or a Valentino or whoever designs these things. I'll have to ask Merrion. She knows all the designer names. Come to think of it, Merrion may be able to get her hands on one for me. She did buy me those beautiful dresses at Christmas, so you never know. Plus she's on friendly terms with almost everyone who is anyone in the fashion industry. I'll have to have a word with her.

But perhaps I should wait until she's in a better mood. Or maybe not. It's time I sat her down and found out exactly what's wrong, even if I have to force it out of her. It's so unlike her to be moody and secretive. She's usually the life and soul of the party. When she returns from wherever she has gone, I'll make her talk to me. I know she's not working today but whilst the rest of us were having breakfast I saw Merrion, through the kitchen window, get into her car. It was only about nine and I don't know why she was in such a hurry but she left a cloud of dust in her wake as she sped off down the drive. And probably several layers of rubber from her tyres.

'Was that Merrion?' Dad asked, having joined us a few minutes earlier, cradling a soundly sleeping Lucinda in his arms.

'I believe it was,' Bella confirmed. 'I wonder where she's off to in such a rush.'

'Who? Merrion?' Reece strolled into the kitchen, pushing his glasses in place. 'She very nearly knocked my iPad out of my hands in her haste. I asked why she was dashing about but she told me to mind my own business and to go and blow up something else. Which wasn't terribly nice of her.'

'What you gonna blow up, Reece?' Theo shrieked, dropping his spoon in his cereal and sending a shower of milk over the table.

'Can we help?' Thor added, clearly excited by the prospect.

'No one is blowing up anything,' Bella said, rather more calmly than I would have. 'We were discussing Merrion. Finish your breakfast.'

Ralph didn't say a word but amazingly, he jumped up and grabbed several sheets of paper towel to mop up the spilt milk.

'Perhaps she's gone to see a man about a dog,' Aunt Vicki said, with a rather odd smile stretching across her thin lips and the strangest look in her beady eyes.

'We getting a dog?' Theo and Thor yelled simultaneously, even more excited by this new possibility than that of creating an explosion.

'One each?' Theo asked.

'I want the wolf!' demanded Thor. 'The one that did the big poo.'

'No one's getting a dog,' I told them. 'And if you mean that Irish wolfhound, then absolutely not. It's almost twice your size for one thing and it's as out of control as the two of you, for another.'

But Dad didn't help by informing us that he had had a Great Dane when he was a boy and that it was rather 'wild' and Aunt Vicki suddenly remembered the time it had got loose during one of the annual Christmas parties. As we all listened to their tales of that night I actually felt a lot better about the disastrous tea party. It seems my shambles of an afternoon wasn't the first time that a dog had peed against the newel post and left a steaming deposit in the Great Hall. I just wish they'd remembered it earlier. But that got us on to the subject of the former, wonderful parties that were once held at The Hall each year. And this then moved on to detailed descriptions of the glorious balls. And that's when I realised I needed a ball gown.

Now, a couple of hours later, I'm sitting in the kitchen on my own and the table is covered with post-it-notes. Little yellow reminders of each phone call I've got to make, every item I need to source, or all the things I have to do. I've got the main list on my iPad but these additional prompts may help and somehow it feels so much better being able to screw up a little piece of paper and toss it in the recycling bin when I can check a detail off my list.

Ralph and Aunt Vicki have gone into the attic to search for the boxes containing her ball gowns. I offered to go with Ralph instead because the stairs to the attic are fairly steep and narrow, but Aunt Vicki assured me she would be fine. I got the impression she was quite looking forward to it. Of course, she will be sitting in one of the discarded chairs up there and merely giving instructions. Ralph will be doing the searching.

Dad and Bella have taken the twins and Lucinda in the rather snazzy new pram that Lance got for them for a walk into the village. It's a beautiful spring day and the footpath through our apple orchard and parkland comes out, via an iron gate, onto a cobbled street at the top of Hall's Cross. Amongst the many types of tree between The Hall's apple orchard and the village, are several other varieties of fruit bearing trees, most of which are in full bloom as we are nearing the end of May, so it's a wonderful path to take. Bella's favourite tree is the cherry and there are a number of those in our grounds. But my favourite, other than a Christmas tree of course (and we do have a great many pine trees) is the Magnolia. We have at least four different colours of those. The deep, rich damson coloured are the ones that make the most impact but they're all glorious in their own way. In early spring, crocus and daffodil compete for space along the footpath almost as far as the eye can see, but now it's tulips and English bluebells that carpet much of the surrounding earth.

I almost wish I'd gone for that walk, but as I told Dad and Bella, I have lots to do, and Gwen called earlier to say she will be popping round to discuss the menu, so I had to stay here and wait for her. Besides, as picturesque as the scenery may be, Theo and Thor were with them, so even if Lucinda sleeps soundly the entire way there and back, the walk would hardly be idyllic.

Bright sunshine pours in through the two large kitchen windows facing the front lawn and drive and I close my eyes and tilt my head skywards, allowing the warmth from the rays to penetrate my skin. I could sit outside in the kitchen garden with its winding path leading to the apple orchard and onward to the woods. There are a couple of tables and chairs and two benches placed here and there; some in full sun, some in shade. Bella likes to sit in the sun, listening to the buzzing of bees as they go about their business, and breathing in the scents of lavender, rosemary and the many other prolific herbs vying for space amongst the borders and the polytunnels containing vegetables, soft fruit and Bella's plant-cuttings. Dad prefers to sit in the shade and read his newspaper. Aunt Vicki likes to watch the birds and other wildlife occupying the woods and the twins like to climb the trees and cause as much chaos as possible. Merrion, Ralph and I often sit out there in the evening with a glass of wine, and Reece – well the only time Reece goes outside is when we make him, or when he needs something from one of the various sheds. Most of the time he's either in his room or in the cellars mixing chemicals and trying not to blow things up. At least he says he tries not to. It's a beautiful garden and the perfect place to be on a day like this. But there's a very slight breeze and as sticky as my post-it notes are, I don't want them flying off in all directions like square butterflies with newly found wings.

'Day dreaming?' I recognise Lance's voice immediately and can tell from the tone that he's smiling. 'I thought you said you were snowed under with all the things you've got to do.'

I open my eyes and smile back. 'I was concentrating on a particular problem.'

'Of course you were.'

He pours himself a large mug of coffee and waves an empty mug for me.

'Help yourself,' I say, grinning. 'And yes please. I'd love a cup of coffee. There's coffee and walnut cake too. If you want some.'

He laughs. 'I assume that's your way of telling me to cut you a slice. Who made it?'

'Bella. So it's delicious.'

He glances round at me. 'How did Bella find the time or energy to make a cake?'

'Bella's a superwoman. Surely you know that

by now?' She is. I truly wish I could be like her.

Lance cuts two slices of cake and somehow manages to bring two plates and two mugs to the kitchen table without spilling a drop of coffee.

'Why aren't you at work?' I ask.

He shrugs. 'The sun's shining, the birds are singing, it's a glorious day. I thought I'd take time out to smell the roses. And to kiss my girlfriend. But she wasn't in so I thought I'd come and see you instead.'

'Oh ha ha.' I throw a pad of post-it notes at his head.

He winks at me and leans across the table to kiss me on the top of my head.

'That's it? Call that a kiss? Surely you can do better than that?'

'I can try,' he says, and once again there's that wicked look in his eyes as he makes his way around the table. 'Where is everyone?'

'Out. With the exception of Ralph and Aunt Vicki, who are possibly trapped beneath a pile of boxes in the attic. But don't get any ideas. I've got a lot to do and just thinking about how much is involved in organising a ball is giving me a headache. Look at all these post-it notes.'

'I have a remedy for headaches,' he says.

He gently pulls me to my feet and leans me against the kitchen table, kissing me, and suddenly post-it notes are the last thing on my mind.

Unfortunately, I had entirely forgotten about Reece, but thankfully, although Lance and I are a little dishevelled, we are still fully clothed when he saunters into the kitchen, his head virtually buried in his iPad. We quickly separate and try to pretend we are studying my notes. Reece seems oblivious, as always.

'Hello Reece,' Lance says, as my stepbrother passes us by.

'Oh, hello Lance. I didn't see you there.' Reece heads towards the door leading to the kitchen garden, his eyes focused once again on his iPad. 'I'm not sure if you are aware, Hairy, but there are several post-it notes stuck to your skirt. How they can possibly be of use there I have no idea. It seems a jolly odd place to stick them.'

The door closes slowly behind Reece and Lance grins at me.

'Let me help you with those post-it notes,' he says, but that's not exactly what he means.

Chapter Fourteen

I'm still thinking about Lance, long after he's left. I can't believe how much I love that man. Or how much he loves me. I really am the luckiest woman in the world. Yet there is still quite a lot I don't know about him. Every time I ask about his past, he tells me it's dead and buried and that the future is all that matters. That's as may be, but sometimes I wonder if he has something to hide. But that's just my imagination running riot, as usual.

I know his parents are dead. His mum passed away eight years ago when Gwen was only ten, which must have been awful for all of them. His dad died four years ago of a heart attack and it makes him sad to talk about either, so we don't. Having lost my mum to cancer more than fifteen years ago now, I totally understand how difficult it is, but I hope in time he will be able to tell me more about the happy times they shared, and not dwell on the sadness of their loss. I know he feels their deaths had an even more devastating effect on

Gwen, and perhaps that explains why she got involved with Jackson Hunter. Again, Lance says he would rather not discuss the past, and maybe he's right. Maybe the future is all that matters.

'Hi,' Gwen says, dragging me out of my thoughts as she pokes her head around the door to the kitchen garden. 'Reece told me to come in this way. I hope that's okay. I bumped into him outside. He's digging a hole in the front lawn. What's he up to now?'

'Is he? The last time I saw him he was heading towards where you're standing now, so I haven't the faintest idea what he's up to, but yes, of course, it's okay. Come in. Would you like some coffee?'

She waves a bottle of white wine in the air. 'I'd prefer some of this and I hope you'll join me. It is lunchtime, after all.'

'Is it?' I look at my watch and see it's twelve-forty-five. 'God. I thought it was only about eleven o'clock. I don't know where today's going. I'd love some wine. I'm not sure what we're having for lunch but Dad and Bella should be back soon. They went to the village this morning but they've been gone for hours... unless they came back and used the front doors. And I haven't seen Ralph and Aunt Vicki since breakfast. I hope nothing's happened to them. Sorry, I'm rambling. They went up into the attic to look for ball gowns.'

Gwen laughs and shakes her head. 'As you do. I'm always looking in Lance's attic for ball gowns but there's nothing up there except spiders.'

'We've got several of those too.' I shake at the thought of them. I really don't like spiders.

'Should we go and check on them?'

'The spiders?'

'No.' Gwen laughs even more. 'Ralph and Aunt Vicki.'

'Oh. That might not be a bad idea. Although it is a very big attic and I'm sure Aunt Vicki is making Ralph search every inch of it.'

No sooner have I finished that sentence than a very dusty looking Ralph marches into the kitchen from the direction of the Great Hall and heads towards the fridge.

'I need a beer and then I need a shower,' he says. 'Oh. Hello Gwen. You're looking lovely.'

'Thank you. So are you.' She laughs louder and moves out of his way. 'Dust and white dresses don't go together.'

He grins at her and winks. 'So does that mean you don't want me to come and kiss you on the cheek?'

'That's exactly what it means.'

'Beer, anyone?' he offers, still grinning.

'We have wine,' Gwen says, holding up the bottle in her hand. 'But we need glasses.'

'To see the wine?'

'Very funny, Ralph. Not those sort of glasses.'

He puts his beer on the kitchen worktop, gets two glasses from the cupboard and hands them to Gwen with a smile.

'By the way, Harri,' he says, giving me a

serious look. 'Next time Aunt Vicki wants something from the attic, you can go and look for it.'

'That bad?' I smile up at him.

'You do realise we've been up there for over three hours, don't you?'

'I do now. But did you find her ball gowns? That's the important thing.'

'We found enough for her to open her own shop and sell the damn things. She insisted I carry every single one of them to her room. Boxes and boxes of them. I'll tell you something. It's not going to be me who takes them all back to the attic.'

'I'd quite like to see them,' Gwen says. 'Do you think she would let me?'

'Let's go and ask her,' I say. 'But perhaps we should have a glass of wine first. We may be there for quite a while if there are as many gowns as Ralph says.'

'It wasn't just gowns,' he adds. 'Did you know there's an entire chest full of jewellery up there?'

'Like a treasure chest?' Gwen asks, her dark eyes wide with excitement.

Ralph tuts. 'No. An upright chest. Like a chest of drawers except the drawers are slimmer. It's full of tiaras, necklaces, stuff like that. She said she had forgotten about it. Can you believe that? I wonder if they're worth anything. They're probably made of glass, knowing this family's finances.'

'I didn't know.' I am surprised but he's probably right. 'They no doubt are made of glass.'

Gwen still looks excited. 'Did you bring that down too?'

'Not the actual chest. But she did make me bring down every single drawer.'

'I quite like the idea of wearing a tiara,' I say. 'Even if it is made of glass.'

'So do I,' says Gwen. 'I wonder if I can persuade her to let me borrow one.'

'Get Lance to ask,' I tell her. 'Aunt Vicki is like putty in his hands.'

Aunt Vicki isn't the only one who is like putty in that man's hands. I turn to goo the minute he looks at me. But I don't tell Gwen that. That's probably a little too much information. Instead, I take the glass of wine Gwen hands to me and think about just how much in love I am with her gorgeous, sexy, big brother.

Chapter Fifteen

Unfortunately, but not surprisingly, most of the tiaras, necklaces, brooches, clasps, bracelets and rings are glass, crystal at best, and paste. The originals which were worth a fortune, would have been sold off by various ancestors long ago. But one or two do contain a few precious stones and Aunt Vicki can tell the difference just by looking at them.

She is happy for me and Gwen to try them on; in fact she encourages us to, and when I spot one of the ball gowns, which is so beautiful that it takes my breath away, she insists I also try that on. As I do so she sifts through another couple of boxes and finds an equally beautiful gown.

'This might suit you, Gwendoline,' she says.

She tosses it to Gwen who willingly takes it, and we spend the next hour or so parading to and fro in Aunt Vicki's bedroom, wearing various gowns and jewels. I thought I wouldn't want to be seen dead in something Aunt Vicki had worn many, many years ago, but she had exquisite taste and several of the gowns wouldn't look amiss in the windows of the classiest boutiques and designer stores.

I spot Merrion walk past the door and am about to call her name but she reappears in the doorway before I get a chance.

'What's going on?' She scans the pile of gowns strewn over Aunt Vicki's bed, the Ottoman at the foot of it, the dressing table chair and the armchair at the window. 'Have you been shopping?'

'No,' I say. 'These were in the attic. They're Aunt Vicki's ball gowns. Some of them are really gorgeous. And very fashionable. I had no idea they would be so beautiful.'

'Or that they might fit,' Merrion says, looking me up and down. 'That one could have been made for you. It suits you, too. You've always looked good in emerald green, and silk and taffeta never go out of fashion. Are you wearing a push-up bra? Or is it the shape of the gown?'

'It must be the gown.' She seems a lot happier now and I smile at her. 'You come and try some on. Look. We have tiaras too. And other jewels. They're not real, so don't get excited. Well, most of them aren't.'

She hesitates for a moment but Merrion loves clothes as much as she loves fast cars so it doesn't take her many seconds to succumb to temptation.

Before long we're parading around the room, one behind the other with Aunt Vicki telling us to 'put your shoulders back', 'stretch your necks more', 'hold your heads higher', 'stick your chests out', and various other commands.

To be honest, Gwen and I are having difficulty simply walking in a straight line, but that may be due to the wine we consumed earlier. Merrion, of course, is a natural when it comes to modelling and has no trouble with any of it.

The thing that amazes all of us though is that virtually every gown we try on, fits us almost to perfection. A few might need a nip and tuck here and there and, height-wise, they are all too long for me, but other than that, Merrion is right. These gowns could have been made for us. It seems the three of us are not only of an almost identical dress size, we are the same size as Aunt Vicki was throughout her teenage years and her twenties.

'Well,' Aunt Vicki says, a hint of sadness in her eyes, 'it seems the only one of us who may be needing a new gown, is me. These are all far too big for my frail bones.'

'You could have one altered to fit,' I point out.

'In four weeks? There are no dressmakers that I know of in the vicinity,' she says. 'Bella could do it of course, but she has more than enough on her plate at the moment with little Lucinda. I have no intention of adding to her burden by asking her to put her sewing skills to use.'

'What about Jodie?' Merrion suggests.

'Ralph's barmaid!' The horror in Aunt Vicki's voice is evident but the look in her eyes emphasises it. 'Have you seen that girl's tattoos? And her nails? Or talons to be more precise. If you are seriously suggesting that I let a girl, who is chewing gum every time I have seen her in the village, loose on my wardrobe, you are deluded at the very least.'

'What have her tattoos or her nails got to do with anything, Aunt?' I ask, slightly bewildered. 'The gum, I understand, but you could ask her not to chew anything when she is working on your clothes.' I glance at Merrion. 'I didn't know Jodie was good with a needle.'

Merrion smirks. 'I think that depends on the needle, but as far as I know she's not. What I was going to say was that I think her mum has done some sewing for a couple of people in the village. Ralph could ask Jodie.'

'Oh,' Aunt Vicki says somewhat more calmly. 'That's a different matter. Unless the mother also chews gum. Or has tattoos.'

'Why does it matter if she has tattoos?' Gwen asks.

'I don't like tattoos and that's an end to it. If the woman has tattoos, she will not be working for me.'

None of us understands this logic, but then Aunt Vicki does have some very strange ideas.

'I don't think she has tattoos,' Merrion says. 'And I'm pretty sure she doesn't chew gum. Shall I ask Ralph to ask Jodie? About the sewing I mean, not the other stuff.'

'I suppose it wouldn't hurt,' Aunt Vicki says, magnanimously. 'And there he is. Ralph! Ralph, my boy. We need you.'

Ralph pokes his head around the door and lets out a long and weary sigh. 'I've had a shower and I'm off to the village. If you want me to put any of this lot back or bring anything else down, it'll have to be later. Much later. I'm going to meet Jodie and I may be some time.'

'Excellent.' Aunt Vicki waves her hand to call him to her. 'That's exactly what I wanted to hear.'

Ralph looks astonished. 'But you don't like Jodie, Aunt. You've never had a nice word to say about her.'

'Of course I don't. But Merrion tells me the girl's mother may be adept with a needle, so I want you to ask her if her mother can sew. And if she can, ask her to come and see me. The mother, that is. Not your barmaid.'

'I didn't know Aunt Vicki didn't like Jodie,' I whisper to Merrion. 'I'm sure she was the one who told me Ralph had a crush on Jodie in the first place.'

'I think I was the one who told you,' she whispers back. 'Aunt Vicki probably mentioned it, but as Ralph says, I doubt it was in a good way.'

'Is it because she's a barmaid? Or is it the tattoos?'

Merrion shrugs. 'Aunt Vicki's your blood relative, not mine. You should know her better than I do. But I think it's because Jodie was in a relationship with someone until very recently but was stringing Ralph along in the meantime. Possibly keeping her options open.'

'It doesn't sound as if you like her very much either.'

'I don't know her that well. She's okay, but I don't think she's right for Ralph and she's not the sort of person we want joining our family.'

'Merrion. I never thought you were a snob.'

'I'm not! It's got nothing to do with what she does and I rather like her tattoos. It's got more to do with the things she does. She seems to flirt with every man in the pub. And I don't simply mean the harmless type of flirting that's tongue-in-cheek. I mean the serious kind. I've even seen her flirt with Lance. I don't like women who do that.'

'Perhaps she's just being friendly.'

'Hmm.' Merrion looks me in the eye. 'There's friendly, Harri, and then there's *friendly*. You should go to the village pub more often. You might see what I mean.'

'What are you two whispering about?' Aunt Vicki asks.

Merrion grins. 'We were just discussing birds, Aunt. And whether we should have some tattoos done. I rather fancy a colourful little blue tit, right here in the middle of my chest.'

Now that's the Merrion I know and love. The one who enjoys winding people up. The one who says what she thinks, but always with a smile. Even if, for just one second, it looks as though

Aunt Vicki might not live to see her ninetieth birthday and we may need to call a paramedic. Her shriek is far, far louder than any we have heard from dear little Lucinda. But of course, she's fine, and soon has a few choice words for Merrion. And there's a smile on Merrion's face that I haven't seen for quite some time.

Chapter Sixteen

I lean against Lance's truck and through the open window, run my finger up and down his bare forearm. He's sitting at the wheel and Thunder is curled up on the seat, next to him.

Lance dropped by on his way home from the job he was working on to tell me that last night he spoke to a guy in the pub about the champagne flutes and the engraving. It seems, as always, he can get it for a very good price and he wanted me to give the go-ahead. Naturally, I did, although I suggested he also checked with Gwen, but that's one thing I can take off my list and one post-it note for the recycling.

He is about to leave but I stop him.

'Does Jodie flirt with you?' I ask, tilting my head to one side and surreptitiously looking at him beneath my lashes.

'Where did that come from?' He seems genuinely surprised.

'I was just wondering. Does she?'

'Jodie from the pub?'

'Yes.'

He shrugs nonchalantly. 'It depends what you mean by "flirt". If you mean does she run her finger up and down my arm and get me all excited, like you are now, then no. But if you mean, does she smile suggestively and make a few risqué remarks, then yes. Sometimes.'

I stop what I'm doing and rest my hand on the open window but he grabs it and kisses my fingers.

'What's this about? Why the sudden interest in Jodie?'

'Do you like her?'

'Jodie?'

'Yes of course, Jodie.'

'Yes. But not in the way I think you mean. Are you jealous? Because you have absolutely no reason to be. Oh, is this because she and Ralph may have finally got together and you're worried about him?'

I nod. 'Sort of. Merrion told me that Jodie's a flirt. Aunt Vicki dislikes her because she has tattoos and chews gum. Oh, and because she has excessively long nails.'

'All very good reasons to dislike someone.'

'Don't laugh.'

'I'm sorry, darling, but honestly.' He's laughing and shaking his head. 'I love your aunt but she's crazy at times. Jodie's a bit wild, but that's not necessarily a bad thing. Ralph could probably do with a bit of 'wild' in his life. I know he's fancied her for ages but I don't think there's any risk of him falling deeply in love. They're like chalk and cheese. They have absolutely nothing in common. Oh wait, that's not true. They both like beer.'

I slap his arm. 'This is serious, Lance.'

'No, Harriet. It isn't. Besides, Jodie has just come out of one serious relationship. I can't see her jumping straight into another.'

'How can you say that? People fall in love all the time. I was in a serious relationship when I met you. I jumped straight out of that one into this.'

'That's true.' He frowns for a moment then leans over and kisses me. 'But that was love at first sight. That's completely different. Ralph has known Jodie since she moved to the pub to be near her boyfriend. Ex-boyfriend, I should say. He lives next door.'

'To you?'

'No. To the pub.' He laughs again. 'You do know that Jodie is the landlord's niece, don't you? She got the flat above the pub when her uncle and aunt moved to the Old Mill House at the other end of the village. Her parents live in Eastbourne.'

'You seem to know a lot about her.'

He winks at me. 'It's the village pub. People talk. You should go there more often. No. *We* should go there more often.'

'Let's go tonight. All of us. You and me. Gwen. Ralph and Merrion.'

'What about Reece?'

Now it's my turn to laugh. 'Reece? In the village pub? I don't think so. For one thing, he's only fifteen and for another, he'd probably manage to mix some chemical with the alcohol and blow the place up.'

'True. Shall I pick you up at eight?'

I shake my head. 'We'll see you there. I've been stuck indoors for most of the day trying on ball gowns and tiaras. I could do with a walk and I'm sure Merrion and Ralph won't mind.'

'Ball gowns and tiaras?'

'Aunt Vicki's. Ralph got them down from the attic. Much to everyone's surprise, most of them are simply gorgeous. We've each chosen one for the ball. Gwen has too. She was with us.'

'I can't wait to see Ralph in his.'

I playfully slap him again. 'You know I didn't mean Ralph had chosen one. Now go away. I'll see you in the pub tonight.'

'Okay,' he says. 'I'll be at the bar flirting with Jodie.' He blows me a kiss and starts the engine.

'Not if you want to come back here and stay the night you won't.'

'In that case you'll find me, Gwen and Thunder, sitting quietly in the corner.' He smiles, winks and pulls away but he stops before he's gone more than a metre and sticks his head out of the open window. 'I love you Harriet,' he says. Then he roars off down the drive before I have a chance to reply.

Chapter Seventeen

I've only been to The Cross in Hand a few times since I returned home last December. Before I went away Ralph, Merrion and I used to come here often, but now I prefer to have a glass of wine or a cocktail at home with my family, or at Lance's house. I'm not really sure why because it's a typically quaint and quintessential English village pub and it's probably been here for as long, if not longer, than The Hall. The staff are welcoming and the clientele are friendly, but it's the only pub in Hall's Cross and it's not particularly large. Even with only twenty or so customers there's not much space to move. There's a fire burning in the inglenook despite the fact that it's a warm evening and in a few days it will be June. Not that that means anything. I can remember times when we've had fires in July at The Hall. But tonight it's bordering on stifling in here.

'Whose idea was it to light the fire?' I ask, peeling off my cardigan as we head to the table where Lance and Gwen are sitting. Thunder is under the table lapping furiously at a bowl of water.

'I suspect it was Jodie,' Merrion says, whilst Ralph heads towards the bar. 'It means she can wear flimsy, low-cut tops without freezing to death.'

I glance across at Jodie as she flicks her long dark hair behind her ear and leans provocatively towards Ralph, resting her elbows on the bar. The white see-through blouse she's wearing is definitely flimsy and low cut, but if I had a figure like hers I might be tempted to wear something similar.

Lance gets up and smiles.

'Ralph's getting drinks,' I say, and I have no idea why, but I reach up and kiss Lance firmly on the lips.

It's not that I wouldn't normally kiss him. It's simply that I wouldn't usually kiss him quite so intently in front of a pub full of villagers. The wolf whistles and cheers are somewhat inevitable and entirely predictable.

'Hello to you too,' he says, with a smile in his eyes and a huge grin on his lips. 'We should meet in the pub more often.'

Either I'm blushing or the heat from the nearby fire is burning my cheeks to a crisp.

I give a little laugh. 'I just want you to feel appreciated.'

'Oh I do,' he says. 'And a lot more besides.'

And now there's a twinkle in his eyes.

Ralph brings over glasses of wine for Merrion and me and beer for himself. 'Want a top up?'

Lance shakes his head and lifts his half full glass. 'I'm fine thanks.'

'Me too,' says Gwen. 'Did you get my email, Harri? I finished off the menu as soon as I got home this afternoon.'

'Yes. And it looks superb to me. Thanks for doing this. But are you sure you're happy to cover all the costs of the food? Some of those ingredients are going to be pretty expensive. The truffles alone will probably cost a fortune. And lobster's not cheap. Nor is crab. But you know all this better than I do.'

Gwen smiles 'We know people. When you're in the business you can always get a good deal on almost anything. Even truffles, lobster and crab. And yes, I'm more than happy to pay for it. Think of it as an additional present for both Lucinda and Aunt Vicki.'

'Excellent,' Merrion says. 'Harri showed us the menu during dinner and it made the steak pie and mash we were eating seem particularly boring. If we did the catering for this little shindig, it would be cocktail sausages and stuffed eggs.'

We all laugh at that. It wouldn't be quite that bad but truffles and lobster would definitely not be on our menu. I'm not even sure we could stretch to crab. Chicken liver parfait would probably be as upmarket as we would get.

'I rather like stuffed eggs,' Ralph says. 'Oh, by the way, I had a quick word with Jodie. Her mum does take on sewing jobs. I said it would only be a few alterations and she's given me her mum's phone number. I'll text it to you.'

He does so immediately and I enter it into my phone under *Jodie's mum.*

'That's four things I can cross off the list: the food, the champagne flutes, our ball gowns, and finding someone to do the alterations. Although perhaps those last two should only count as one.'

Merrion laughs. 'And how many more are there to go? Only about three hundred from what I saw.'

'Don't exaggerate,' I say. 'It's nowhere near that amount. But there is still an awful lot to do.'

'Anything else we can help with?' Lance offers. 'I told you I'll sort out all the outside lights and the flame torches you wanted. I spoke to Ophelia this evening and she says she'll provide the flowers from the florist who does all the arrangements at her restaurant.'

'Wow. Really? Those arrangements are magnificent. And are you sure about the lights and torches?'

He nods. 'Yep. I know a man...' He doesn't bother to finish the sentence and merely smiles.'

'That will be etched on your gravestone,' Merrion says.

'Not for many, many years to come, I hope.'

I lean in and kiss him on his cheek. 'I hope so

too.'

'Oh look,' Gwen says. 'There's Dan.'

'Dan!' Merrion spills her wine down her dress and her face drains of colour, even with the heat of the fire. 'Shit.' She dabs at her dress with the tissue I hand her. 'I need to go.'

'No you don't.' Ralph grabs her arm as she starts to get to her feet and forces her to sit back down. 'I have no idea why you dislike this guy so much but the sister I know and love doesn't run away from anyone or anything.'

'He's right, Merrion,' I add. 'And besides, it's not as if he's going to be joining us… Oh dear. I think he's coming over.'

Lance gives her an odd look and stands up. 'If you really can't stand the guy, I'll head him off and take him to the bar. I'll get us more drinks while I'm there.'

'Thanks,' she says, 'but Ralph's right. I can handle this.' She takes a deep breath and empties the remains of her wine glass in one long gulp before handing the empty glass to Lance. 'A large one, please.'

Lance steps in front of the approaching Dan. 'Hi, Dan. What would you like? I'm getting them in. Give me a hand, will you?'

Dan looks a little surprised but a smile quickly appears. 'Oh okay. Hi everyone.' He gives us all a little wave and goes to the bar with Lance.

Merrion doesn't move a muscle. She's got her back to him so I don't know if Dan has spotted her but with her blonde hair and fabulous figure, she's difficult to miss, even from the back view.

'It's none of my business,' Gwen says, 'but why don't you like Dan? He seems a really nice guy.'

'Looks can be deceiving. And you're right. It is none of your business.'

'Merrion.' I'm surprised she snapped at Gwen.

'Sorry.'

Gwen smiles at her. 'No problem. I know what it's like when people poke their noses into other people's business. I didn't mean to pry. You clearly know something we don't.'

'No she doesn't,' I say. 'She met him for the first time when we got back from the hospital and he and Lance were searching for the last of the escaped dogs.'

'That wasn't the first time,' Merrion says.

'What? You already knew him?' I can't believe this. 'How? You didn't behave as if you knew one another.'

'I don't think he remembered me.'

Now that I don't believe. 'Oh come on, Merrion. No one ever forgets you.'

'He clearly has. But don't you dare say a word.' She looks a little frantic as she glares at us. 'I mean it. Not one word.'

'Okay,' Ralph says. 'But I want to hear all about it the minute we get home.'

'Same here,' I add.

Gwen doesn't say anything. She merely sips

her wine and stares in the direction of the fire. Until Lance returns with the drinks... and Dan. 'Hi, Dan.'

'Hi, Gwen. Hi, everyone.'

Merrion doesn't acknowledge him but Ralph and I smile and return his friendly greeting.

'Is it okay if I join you? I've only lived in Hall's Cross for about two weeks so I'm still getting to know people.'

'And yet you've found yourself a girlfriend.' Merrion still doesn't look at him. 'Or have you dumped her already?'

He sits in the vacant seat next to Ralph, diagonally opposite Merrion's. 'I haven't dumped anyone. And going on one date with someone hardly makes them my girlfriend. You know that better than me.'

Merrion glares at him. 'Is there going to be a second?'

He stares back at her. 'I wasn't sure until tonight. But yes, I think there is. And a third. Who knows where it may lead.'

She sneers. 'Lucky girl.'

'No. Lucky me. Just in the right place at the right time. You know how that works.'

'Um.' Lance holds up his hand. 'Excuse me, guys, but is there something going on between you two?'

'Absolutely not!' Merrion grabs the glass Lance brought her and knocks back the contents.

'Not a hope in hell's chance,' Dan says, and

gulps down his beer.

'Well,' Ralph says. 'This is going to be a fun evening, isn't it?'

Dan empties his glass and gets to his feet. 'I can't stay. I only popped in for a quick drink. Thanks Lance. Next time it's on me. Bye, everyone. It was lovely to see you again, Merrion.'

'Whatever.' She still doesn't look at him.

'You're going?' Gwen sounds as surprised as I'm sure the rest of us feel. 'But you've only just arrived.'

Merrion sneers. 'Quick exits are his speciality. I'm surprised he stayed this long.'

'Yeah. And making a guy feel special is yours. Have a good night.'

'Dan…?' He's gone before I get a chance to ask what he meant by that. So I ask Merrion instead. 'Okay, Merrion. What the hell just happened? What did he mean by that?'

'I need another drink.' She jumps to her feet but I stop her. 'Not before you tell me what on earth is going on between you and Dan?'

'Nothing's going on. Nothing at all. Not a thing.'

'Well, something must've happened between you or that was the weirdest conversation in the history of conversations.'

'You may as well spill,' Lance says.

'Yeah. Come on, sis. What's this all about?' Ralph adds.

She looks at each of us and frowns. 'We met at

a club in London several weeks ago. Had a few drinks. Had a few laughs. Had sex. Thought I was in love. Never heard from him again. Okay? Now I need another drink.'

Merrion heads to the bar whilst we all stare at one another, open mouthed.

Chapter Eighteen

Merrion flatly refuses to discuss last night.

After her revelation, she wouldn't say any more about it when she came back from the bar, and she threatened to go home unless we dropped the subject. So reluctantly, we did. When Lance brought us all home, he offered to go back to his place if I wanted some time alone with Merrion, but she overheard and told him not to bother on her account. The topic was closed and that was that.

I tried again this morning but all she would say was that she regretted telling us and told me to leave well alone.

So I really don't have much choice. Except... there are two sides to every story.

'No,' Lance says emphatically, as I kiss him goodbye in the driveway before he heads off to work. 'Absolutely not. There is no way I am going to ask Dan what happened between him and Merrion. No way. I am not asking a guy I have only recently met about his sex life.'

'I'm not asking you to. You don't have to mention the word sex. All I want to know is why they seem to dislike one another so much. Lots of people hook up for sex but they don't despise each other the next day. You saw them last night. And Merrion mentioned the word "love". She's never said that about anyone. Well, not in that way. Obviously, she loves us. Oh, you know what I mean. I just want to know if he felt anything for her. And why he didn't call her after they spent the night together.'

'Well, if that's all, of course I'll ask him.'

'You will?'

'No, Harriet. I love you and I will do almost anything to make you happy. But I am not going to ask a man I hardly know why he had sex with my girlfriend's sister, and didn't bother to call her again. I don't think we should get involved. They will either sort it out themselves and eventually be civil to one another or they won't. In which case, I think we should avoid the village pub in future. Now I have to go. My men are waiting at the site and I've got to go and pick up my truck first.'

'Have a lovely day.'

He kisses me and looks deep into my eyes. 'You too. What are your plans for the day? Crossing more things off your list, I assume.' He opens the car door and Thunder jumps onto the passenger seat.

'Yes. And deciding what to get Aunt Vicki for her birthday.'

'Any ideas?'

'Ah-huh.' I nod and kiss him again before he gets into his car. 'I'm toying with one idea in particular, but it's a secret.'

He grins and starts the engine. 'Well, good luck. I hope you can find what you want.'

I wave him goodbye. 'So do I,' I mumble, as I watch him drive away. 'I'm going to see a man about a dog.'

Chapter Nineteen

'Hello, Dan. Have you got a minute?'

Dan stops what he's doing and looks up at me.

'Oh. Good morning, Harriet. I didn't expect to see you this morning. How are you?'

'Fine thanks. You?'

'Great. Although preparing dog food the morning after several pints of beer isn't my dream job.'

'You only had one pint.'

He looks directly at me. 'In the pub, maybe. I had a few more when I got home.'

'Do you live here? At the sanctuary I mean?'

'Yeah. The job of manager comes with that cottage.'

He nods in the direction of a nearby, white painted, stone cottage with two windows downstairs, either side of the wood-planked front door, and two windows upstairs, all topped with a thatched roof, which is clearly nearing the end of its useful life.

'Nice.'

'Did you say nice, or mice? Because it seems I'm not the only occupant. I think there are bats in the attic too.'

I can't help but smile. 'I think Aunt Vicki suffers with that.'

He bursts out laughing. 'So what can I do for you, Harriet? And whatever it is, do you mind if we discuss it whilst I work. The animals need feeding and both my staff have called in sick.'

'I can't believe only three of you run this place.'

'Only one today. Unless you fancy giving me a hand.'

'Oh. Um. Well, okay then. Tell me what you want me to do.'

He gives me an odd look. 'I was joking.'

'I wasn't. I've got a couple of hours to spare. I'm happy to help. And it's the least I can do after that disastrous tea party.'

'I thought The Starlight Ball was supposed to be a sort of atonement for that. Not that you have anything to atone for. It really wasn't your fault.'

I shrug. 'I believe in paying one's dues in life. Seriously, what can I do?'

'I can give you a list.' He smiles at me. 'You can help me feed the animals if that's okay?'

'Absolutely.'

'There are some overalls in there.' He points to a metal cupboard with double doors. 'Or jackets if you'd rather wear one of those. Help yourself.

114

They're all clean. I washed them myself only yesterday.'

'A domesticated man. I like that.' I grab a knee-length, dark green, cotton overall which is only a couple of sizes too big.

'Needs must. I've lived alone since my last relationship broke up.'

'When was that?'

He hands me a pile of animal food bowls of varying shapes and sizes. 'Two years ago.'

'How long were you together? And did you dump her or did she dump you?'

He bends down to open a bag of dog food and grins up at me. 'What makes you think it was a she?'

'I just assumed. But I know the saying that one should never assume. Although you did say in the pub last night that you had been on a date with a girl.'

He laughs. 'It was a she. Her name was Julia. We'd been together since uni, but she dumped me for something better.'

'Something better?'

'A better life.' Now he isn't smiling. 'It seems that being with a guy whose sole ambition in life is to work with rescued or abandoned animals, is not many girls' dream. Although Julia left me for a vet, so I suppose she just wanted an upgrade. Better salary, shorter hours, well-cared for pets, generally speaking.'

'I think you're better off without her.'

'Probably.' He begins filling bowls with food and places each of them on an old tea trolley. 'Okay. Can you do the same with the bowls you're holding, please?'

'I think I can manage that.'

'Yeah. It's hardly rocket science.'

'Dan?' I begin my task. 'Did it make you feel… inadequate in some way? Julia dumping you for a vet, I mean.'

'Not inadequate, exactly. But yeah. It made me feel a bit of a loser for a time. Until I remembered I love what I do. And it was my choice to do it. Then I felt okay again until…' His voice trails off.

'Until…?'

He sighs. 'Let's just say that Julia wasn't the only woman to make me feel that way.'

'Other women did the same? I think you're meeting the wrong women, Dan.'

'Only one other woman. But yeah. Definitely wrong. Wrong for me, at least. Perfect in every other way.'

I stop and meet his eyes and we stare at one another for what seems like an eternity, but is only a matter of seconds.

'Dan?'

'Yes?'

'What happened between you and Merrion?'

'Nothing.' He turns away and smashes the tea trolley full of bowls against a door, which immediately swings open.

'Dan?'

'Drop it, Harriet. The last thing I want to talk about today is what didn't happen between me and Merrion.'

'Didn't happen? But I thought… That is…'

He glances back at me. 'Please, Harriet. Not today. And if that's what you came here to talk about, I think you'd better leave.'

'No. No I came to talk about a dog. I'm thinking of getting one for Aunt Vicki's ninetieth.'

He stops and turns. 'A dog? Seriously? You're thinking of adopting a dog for your ninety-year-old aunt.'

'Yes. She likes dogs. We often look after Thunder. That's Lance's dog. And Dad had a dog. And Aunt Vicki's fiancé had a dog. But he died. They both died. The fiancé and then the dog. Aunt Vicki never married because it upset her so much. But now she's ready to try again. With a dog. Not a fiancé.'

Dan throws his head back and laughs. It's a joyful sound and one that makes his face look even more handsome.

'I don't know whether to believe that's really why you came. But if you want a dog, then we have plenty.' He's serious suddenly. 'But a dog is for life, Harriet. Not just for a ninetieth birthday. So I need to be sure that if you take one, he or she is going to a permanent home. No matter what happens.'

'I understand. The dog will have a permanent home. I promise you that. No matter what.'

And much to my surprise, I mean it. Which is odd. Because I didn't really come here for a dog.

Chapter Twenty

When I first tell Dad and Bella that I want to get a dog as a present for Aunt Vicki, my suggestion doesn't go down too well.

'A dog?' Dad says. 'After what happened at the tea party. You believe the one thing Vicki needs most in her life is a dog?'

'Just a little one.'

Bella giggles like a girl. 'I'm sorry, Wyndham darling. I shouldn't laugh. It's a serious matter. But… a little dog might not be so bad. And Theo and Thor would love it. You know they've talked of little else since we brought Lucinda home. They keep asking why they can't have a pet. And we all love Thunder. Perhaps a little dog like Thunder would make our family complete.'

'Our family is complete. We don't need a dog for that. And Theo and Thor have got pets. We have a horse and donkey.'

'Yes darling. But Pegasus and Sirius live in the stables.'

'So would a dog if we had one.'

'Why, Dad? When Thunder stays, he doesn't go to the stables. He either comes upstairs with me and Lance, or sleeps in the kitchen in his bed.'

'Thunder isn't ours.'

'Darling. Why does that make a difference? And another little dog would be company for Thunder. I think it's a good idea. And the more I think about it, the more I wonder if perhaps we should get one for Thor and Theo too.'

'What! Bella darling, don't we have our hands full as it is, with Lucinda and the twins?'

Dad looks as if he may have a heart attack at any moment and I wonder if it was wise to mention a dog at all.

'Calm down, darling,' Bella says. 'Of course things are a tad… frantic at times, at the moment. But having pets of their own would teach the twins responsibility, and that's not such a bad thing. Plus, dogs would keep them occupied.'

'Dogs? Are you now suggesting they have one each? In addition to the one Harriet is proposing to get for Vicki? Three dogs? Three dogs running riot in The Hall? Four, including Thunder.'

'Thunder doesn't run riot,' I say. 'He is very well behaved. Most of the time.'

Bella nods enthusiastically. 'And with training, the other three would be too. We could ask Reece to take charge of that. We might be able to persuade him that it was a different type of experiment. But one not involving any form of chemicals. Or explosions. Reece is very good with animals. He wouldn't want them to come to any harm.'

'Are you intimating that by getting Theo, Thor and Vicki, dogs, we may be able to persuade Reece not to blow things up so often?'

'Yes darling. And possibly not at all. He will be so occupied with the dogs he won't have time for experiments. Hmm. Now that I think about it, perhaps Reece should have one of his own. I don't know why this has never occurred to us before. The Hall is large enough to accommodate four small dogs, and we would probably hardly even notice they were here.'

I'm not really sure what just happened. I came to ask Bella and Dad if there was a slight chance that I could adopt a dog for Aunt Vicki. It was going to be on the basis that, if she didn't want it, I'd have it and take care of it. Somehow we got from one dog to two, then three and I think, but I'm not entirely certain, that Dad and Bella have now settled on four. That will mean that at any given time, if we also include Thunder in the calculation, there could be up to five dogs running around The Hall. Five dogs. That's only three less than we had dashing about at the tea party – and that was utter chaos.

And as Dan reminded me earlier, a dog is for life. It seems we may be having four of them.

I have a feeling I may live to regret this.

Chapter Twenty-One

I lean against Lance's kitchen worktop and watch as he prepares spaghetti bolognese for me, Gwen and himself. I offered to help but Lance enjoys cooking. Clearly it runs in his family. Although anyone can make spaghetti bolognese. Even Reece. But we are never quite sure what Reece puts in his.

'You can open some wine,' Lance says. 'Gwen should be back any minute. She took Thunder for a walk forty minutes ago.'

I grab a bottle from the rack and pour us both a glass.

'You don't happen to know anyone who has a band or plays in one, do you?' I ask, handing Lance his glass.

'For The Starlight Ball, you mean?'

'No. To accompany our supper.'

He grabs a tea towel from the worktop and throws it at me. 'What sort of music?'

I shrug. 'Dance music. It is a ball, after all.'

He takes a deep breath. 'Modern? Swing? Jazz? Hip-hop?'

I raise my eyebrows. 'Hip-hop. Yes. Because Aunt Vicki will love that.'

'She probably would.' He laughs and does a strange little dance.

'And that was…?'

'Don't you appreciate my dance moves?'

'Oh. I thought you were in pain.'

He narrows his eyes but a mischievous smile forms on his lips. 'No. But you may be if you're not careful. So what type of music do you want?'

'What about Strauss?'

'I think you'll find he's dead. Actually… both of them are. Father and son.'

'I meant their music. We can waltz. We can polka. We can quadrille. Does one quadrille? Or does one form a quadrille?'

'And I would know that because…?'

'Oh. I forgot I was dating a virtual philistine.' I smile broadly and he winks at me. 'Anyway. Do you know anyone who plays that type of music?'

'No. But I expect I can find someone who knows someone. Oh. Ophelia probably does. Know someone, I mean. She's had bands perform in her grounds. She's had operas too. Do you want one of those?'

'An opera singer? No. Will you call and ask her, please? I'd love to tick that off my list. I've been searching the internet ever since I got back from the Hall's Cross…' Damn. I hadn't meant to say that. Perhaps he didn't notice.

He did. He stops stirring the bolognese sauce and looks me directly in the eye. 'Since you got back from where?'

I give a little cough, take a sip of wine followed by a deep breath, and smile at him. 'Oh. Didn't I mention it? We may be getting a dog.'

'No, you didn't mention it. We, as in your family?'

I nod. 'Yes.'

'Why?'

'Why not? There are so many abandoned animals who need a good home.'

'I agree. But why the sudden interest? This wouldn't have anything to do with what happened last night between Merrion and Dan, would it?'

I take another sip of wine but I'm saved from an explanation by Gwen and Thunder returning from their walk.

'Hi Gwen. Would you like a glass of wine?'

'I'd love one, Harriet. Thanks. Something smells nice.'

'Spaghetti bolognese,' Lance says. 'The Halls may be getting a dog, Gwen. Did you know anything about this?'

Gwen looks from Lance to me and back again. 'No. It's the first I've heard of it. Is this true?' She smiles at me. 'Are you?'

'Not me, exactly. I'm getting a little one for Aunt Vicki for her birthday.'

'I think that's a lovely idea. Why the long face,

Lance? You love dogs.'

'I do love dogs. I'm just not that keen on my girlfriend interfering in someone else's love life.'

Again, Gwen looks from Lance to me and back again.

'How is getting a dog, interfering in…' The penny clearly drops. 'Oh I see.' She turns her face to me and grins. 'The Hall's Cross Animal Rescue Sanctuary.'

I shrug. 'It's the nearest place.'

Lance looks me directly in the eye. 'A dog is for life, Harriet. Not something to be used. And certainly not as a pawn in some sort of dating game.'

'I know. Don't look at me like that. I've discussed it with Bella and Dad and they think it's a good idea. In fact, they think it is such a good idea, that they've decided that we should get more than one.'

'Really?' Gwen sounds excited. 'So you're getting two dogs?'

I give another little cough. Longer and louder this time. 'Four.'

Lance drops his wooden spoon. It makes a dull thud as it hits the floor and splatters the kitchen units with bolognese sauce.

Chapter Twenty-Two

Lance and I have officially had our first row since we became a couple. Well, perhaps it wasn't a row exactly, but he did lecture me a bit, and he wasn't very happy. He told me that I shouldn't interfere in Merrion and Dan's love lives. And I shouldn't have talked my family into possibly adopting four dogs. Although I'm not really sure that I did. Bella seemed to be doing most of the persuading if my memory serves me correctly. I only wanted to have one dog. But Lance said that I should have known better. He also said that I promised him I wouldn't go to see Dan. I said that I wasn't a child and I could do exactly what I liked. I told Lance where he could stuff his spaghetti bolognese and walked out.

The worst part is, he's probably right. I shouldn't interfere in other people's lives. But naturally, I didn't admit that. And I have just behaved like a child by walking out. I was hoping he would come after me but he hasn't. I'm not sure what to do. Either I go back and apologise, or go home to The Hall and hope it all blows over. Flashing lights, a honking horn and the screech of brakes stops me in my tracks. Unfortunately, I hadn't realised that I'm standing in the middle of the road. But thankfully, it's Merrion who shouts at me from the open window of the Land Cruiser that almost ran me over.

'Shit, Harri! What in God's name are you doing in the middle of the road? I could've killed you.'

'I've had a row with Lance.'

She gets out of the car and comes to me, wrapping her arms around me.

'What about? You were your usual happy, madly in love selves this morning. Is it serious?'

I shake my head. 'I don't know. He shouted at me because we're possibly getting a dog. Well, four dogs actually.'

'Four dogs? Who? You and Lance? I'm sorry, Harri. I'm not following this.'

I shake my head again. 'No. Aunt Vicki, Reece, and Theo and Thor.'

'What! You must be kidding.'

I shake my head some more.

'Will you stop shaking your head and explain.'

'Please don't shout at me, Merrion. I've had enough of that from Lance.'

'I don't blame him. Get in the car. We'll go and sort this out.'

'Harriet?' Gwen calls my name. 'Come back

with me and let's sit down and talk about this.'

My eyes search the fading twilight but Lance is nowhere to be seen.

'Where's Lance? Did he send you to get me?'

She looks a little anxious. 'You know men. They get a bee up their backside and it takes them several hours to work it out. He'll come round.'

'I'm not going back until he does.'

'Are you okay?' a passing motorist stops and shouts from his open window.

'No. My boyfriend and I have had a row.'

The motorist blinks and shakes his head. 'That'll be the least of your worries if you stand in the road. Go and cry on the pavement. Bloody women.' He closes the window and drives away.

'That wasn't very nice,' I say. 'I need a drink.'

Merrion sighs. 'He's a dickhead. But he does have a point. Let's get out of the road before a delivery lorry comes and mows us down. Gwen? Are you coming with us? Or are you going back to Lance's?'

Gwen hesitates for a second. 'I'll come with you.' She runs to the car and climbs onto the back seat.

'Home?' Merrion says. 'Or the pub?'

'The pub,' Gwen and I say in unison and Merrion roars off down the road.

'So tell me what happened,' she says.

'I'm not really sure. One minute Lance is cooking supper and we're discussing music. Everything is fine until I mention we may be getting some dogs. He suddenly gets very serious and starts lecturing about how I need to grow up and think about my actions. And how I shouldn't interfere in people's lives and… and other stuff like that.'

'What did he mean by that? Whose lives have you been interfering in?' She glances at Gwen via the mirror. 'Is this about you?'

'No.' Gwen gives me a questioning look as if to say: 'Are you going to tell your sister or shall I?' But all she says is: 'No. It wasn't about me.'

I clear my throat as Merrion pulls up in the gravel-covered car park of The Cross in Hand.

'Lance thinks I'm trying to interfere in your love life.'

She laughs. 'Well, it's true. You are. But there's no reason for Lance to be angry about that. I don't understand.'

'He's cross because I went to see Dan today. And that's why we're getting the dogs.'

Merrion turns in her seat and glares at me. 'You did what?'

'Now you're cross too.'

'Too right I am. What is the matter with you, Harri?'

I shake my head again. I can feel tears pricking at my eyes and the last thing I want to do now is start blubbing. 'I don't know. I just want us all to be happy.'

'I am happy.'

'You're not.'

Merrion lets out a long sigh. 'No, you're right. I'm not. But we don't live in a land filled with unicorns and rainbows. This is real life, Harri. And sometimes real life sucks.'

'You're telling me,' Gwen says.

Merrion nudges me. 'Come on. Let's all go inside and get drunk. That's what grown-ups do. But I want to know precisely what you said to Dan and what he said to you. Okay?'

'Okay.'

'And I want you to promise that you won't interfere again.'

'I promise.'

Chapter Twenty-Three

'I think Dan may have been talking about you, Merrion,' Gwen says, when I finish telling them everything I can remember about my conversation with Dan.

'No way. I didn't make him feel inadequate, or inferior, or anything else. In fact,' she says, blushing, 'if anything, I think I made him feel pretty special. Several times. If you get what I mean. If anyone was made to feel bad, it was me. When he walked out and didn't call.'

'Why did he walk out?' I ask. 'How did we meet? Did you wake up and find him gone? Did he simply say thanks and leave? What happened?'

Merrion cradles her wine glass in her hand and there's a wistful expression on her face.

'I'm not really sure what happened. We met in a nightclub as I've said. He was standing behind me and when I turned round I spilt my drink down his shirt. I was pretty tipsy and I tried to wipe it off with my hands. Then… I don't know. I looked up into his eyes and wham! It hit me. I felt something I've never felt before. Like I'd known him all my life and yet he was a complete stranger. We didn't say a word for ages. We just stared at one another. The music in the club had been really loud but suddenly I couldn't hear it. All I could hear was our breathing.' She stops and takes several gulps of wine.

'I felt a bit like that when I met Jackson,' Gwen says. 'But that's another story and we don't want to talk about that. Then what happened, Merrion?'

'Actually Gwen,' I say, inappropriately I suppose. 'I would like to hear about you and Jackson. Maybe later?'

She glances at me over her the rim of her wine glass. 'I'll need several more of these before I can talk about Jackson. Let's deal with Merrion's problems first.'

Merrion laughs, but it's a mirthless sound. 'I'm not sure my problem can be solved. Anyway. He took my hand and asked if I wanted to go and get some coffee. I thought it was a euphemism but it wasn't. We actually went and got coffee at the hotel where I was staying. But it was obvious what we both wanted and it wasn't long before we went upstairs to my room.' She runs her hand through her hair. 'It was the best night of my life. I know everyone says that. But it's true. It was. In the morning he asked if I had plans for the day. I told him I had to attend a brief meeting with a colleague but after that I would be free. He said

132

he'd wait. When I came back he was gone. No note. No message left at the desk. No sign of him.'

'That's weird,' I say.

'Very weird,' says Gwen.

'But… Didn't you have his name? His number? Where he worked? Was it a complete surprise when he turned up in Hall's Cross?'

'I knew his name was Dan, but we didn't get as far as surnames. I didn't take his number because I thought he would still be there. And all he said about his work was that he had a temporary job in an animal rescue centre in the outskirts of London but that he would be starting a permanent job fairly soon. I didn't ask where, and he didn't say. So yes, it was a complete surprise when he turned up here.'

Gwen frowns. 'Did you tell him where you lived? Or what you did for a living? Did you tell him about The Hall? Perhaps that's why he felt intimidated.'

'No. Whenever I tell a guy I'm a lip model, they either run, or pile on the sexual innuendos. I said I worked in magazines. Which is sort of true. But I didn't say where I lived or with whom. He did ask if I was single while we were having coffee. I said I was and he said he was too.'

'At least we know that's true. He is single,' I say.

'But dating someone,' Merrion adds, glumly.

'One date so far,' Gwen says.

I lean back in my seat. 'I just don't get it. He

seemed really nice today. Open and friendly. Not the sort of guy who would behave like that. And why did he seem so cross with you? I now understand why you were so unpleasant to him.'

'Thanks.'

'Well, you were. But if all you were to him was a one-night stand then why get so cross when he saw you again?'

'Perhaps,' Gwen says. 'Because he realised you and he were going to be neighbours of sorts. Maybe he doesn't want people to know about his sex life. Do we know who the girl he's dating is?'

'No idea,' I say, and Merrion shakes her head.

'Then that's what we need to find out.'

'How does that help Merrion?' I ask.

'It probably doesn't,' Gwen says. 'But I feel we need to know. In the meantime, I'll get more drinks.' She glances towards the bar, and suddenly turns deathly pale. 'Oh... My... God. It's Jackson.'

Merrion and I look frantically around but we can't see anyone resembling Jackson Hunter. Not even vaguely. I follow Gwen's line of sight and realise she's staring at the TV at the other end of the pub. Which of course isn't very far away because The Cross in Hand isn't large. Merrion must have seen it too because she shouts at Jodie to turn up the volume.

'Jackson Hunter,' the news reporter says, 'arguably one of the best footballers of our time, has signed a seven-figure deal to write his memoirs.'

'Memoirs?' Merrion says. 'The guy's only just turned twenty-six!'

Gwen drops down on her seat and doesn't say a word.

Merrion's ranting about how so-called celebrities shouldn't be allowed to write memoirs until they're old enough to have something interesting to say. And how no one wants to read about a bastard like Jackson Hunter, anyway. But we all know that people do, and they'll no doubt buy his book by the lorry-load.

I'm starting to get worried about Gwen. She hasn't said a word since she sat back down and there's a strange look in her eyes. It's almost as if she's in some sort of trance and I'm not sure what to do.

Lance appears from nowhere. 'Thank God I've found you.'

His voice sounds fraught and his eyes look frantic. I think he's speaking to me, but I realise he's looking at Gwen.

'Are you okay?' he continues. 'I assume by the look on your face you've seen the news. I heard it on the radio. Let's get you home.'

Gwen doesn't reply. Lance walks past Merrion's seat and with one arm around Gwen, lifts his sister to her seemingly unsteady feet, which appears to bring her out of it.

'Lance.' She's clearly surprised he's there but her voice is soft and somehow distant. 'Oh. When did you get here?'

'A moment ago. I'm taking you home.'

'Oh okay. But I'm fine.' She glances at me and Merrion. 'Can Harriet and Merrion come?'

Frankly, she sounds weird but Lance finally looks at me and he seems less worried now.

'I'm sorry I behaved like a tyrant, Harriet. Will you and Merrion come back with us?' A smile appears. 'There's plenty of spaghetti bolognese.'

'I love spaghetti bolognese,' Merrion says. 'I'm in if Harri is.'

'Absolutely.' I feel as if a heavy weight has been lifted from my heart. 'I'm sorry I behaved like a child.'

'No,' he says. 'It was my fault. I behaved like a bully. I was on my way to The Hall to apologise when I heard this news and then I saw Merrion's car and thought you might all be here. I'd like to get Gwen home.'

Chapter Twenty-Four

By the time Merrion and I reach Lance's house, Gwen is back to her normal self, whatever that may be. She and Lance had returned home in his car and I came in Merrion's. I got a feeling Lance wanted some time alone with his sister and clearly, whatever he said must have worked. She is smiling and pouring wine when Merrion and I walk into the kitchen.

'Here,' she says, handing glasses to me, Merrion and Lance. 'Cheers.' She raises hers in the air. 'Here's to the future and whatever it may hold.'

'I'll drink to that,' Merrion says.

'You'll drink to anything,' Lance points out as he clinks glasses with me and smiles.

'I won't be drinking to the success of Jackson bloody Hunter's book,' she says, and for one second, it feels as if time has stopped and we're all holding our breaths.

Gwen laughs and we breathe again.

137

'I know we shouldn't wish ill on anyone,' she says. 'But I hope his book's a massive flop. Unlike a certain appendage of his which was on a perpetual high.'

I almost choke on my mouthful of wine. I'm dying to ask, but I don't. Luckily, I don't have to. Gwen's obviously over her shock and wants to spill her guts, a bit like Jackson will be in his upcoming book.

'I wonder if he'll be honest about all the other women he slept with between our honeymoon and our separation. That alone could fill a book.'

'Men are never honest about stuff like that,' says Merrion. 'They either exaggerate in the hope of making themselves seem like some kind of stallion, or they deny everything in the hope of convincing their girlfriends or wives that there will never be anyone else for them.'

'Not all men are like that,' I say, glancing at Lance and hoping that there really won't be anyone else for him.

Gwen empties her wine glass and pours herself another.

'Do you know that in the few months we were together he never once told me he loved me? Not once. Not even when he proposed. Not even in our marriage vows. And what a joke they were. The ink on the certificate was barely dry before his eye was wandering to pastures new.'

'Are you sure you want to talk about this, Gwen?' From the look in his eyes, Lance is concerned.

'Yes,' she says emphatically. 'And I may as well tell my side of the story before it's plastered across every internet-connected device in the country, courtesy of my dearly beloved husband.'

She reaches for the wine bottle but Lance gets there first.

'Slow down,' he says. 'A sore head in the morning is the last thing you need.'

'Dear Lance. Always looking out for me. I should have listened to you. You told me to wait a few months. To think about it. But I didn't listen. I made my bed and every other woman on the planet got to lie in it.' She grins. 'Until I set it on fire.'

Now I do choke on my wine. I didn't know she had done that.

'Is… Is that why you were arrested?'

Lance looks at me but he doesn't say a word.

'Oh no,' Gwen says, casually waving her arm in the air as if setting fire to beds is an everyday occurrence. 'He told the police and firefighters that it was an accident. That a lighted candle had fallen onto the duvet – which was true, it had, but not by accident. I was arrested because the following day he gave me a cast iron pan as 'a make-up present'. It was a wonderful pan, but it didn't really say: 'I love you and I promise I'll never sleep with another woman again.' Something inside me flipped.'

I'm almost afraid to ask but I can't help myself. 'What did you do?'

She screws up her face and then looks remorseful. 'I hit him with it, and while he was unconscious, I trashed the house – his house. I threw all his clothes onto the massive compost heap at the end of the vegetable garden, tossed every one of his electronic devices into the swimming pool, and finally, I superglued the pan to the crotch of his jeans. It was only then that I realised he hadn't come to and that I might have actually killed him. I called an ambulance and waited.'

'Luckily,' Lance says, 'Jackson pulled through. He was out for about an hour and the doctors were initially concerned, but the guy must have a head made of iron because he was fine within a few hours. And he did the second decent thing he's ever done. He told the police he'd fallen and hit his head and he didn't press charges over his wrecked house. Gwen got away with a warning and a promise to me that she'd get some professional help to make sure nothing like that ever happens again. We'd moved down here to get away from the hustle and bustle of London, so Gwen came back to live with me. Your family helped us a great deal in those early days and the media attention finally died down.'

'I saw a shrink for a time,' Gwen says. 'And it hasn't happened since. Although I will advise all future boyfriends to buy me flowers, not kitchen equipment if we have a row.'

Chapter Twenty-Five

Gwen's revelations really surprised me, but I suppose none of us ever knows how we will react in certain situations, or what it might take to make us 'flip' as Gwen had. I'm glad I finally know. Especially as media attention may resurface because of Jackson's book. Forewarned is forearmed. Isn't that the saying?

What I'm most pleased about though is that Lance and I made up. We made up a lot. For most of the night, in fact. So much so, that I'm tempted to spend today in bed. I can't of course. There is still a very long list to get through if The Starlight Ball is going to be a success.

Lance and Gwen have sorted the invitations, so that's another thing I can cross off. Bella, Aunt Vicki, Merrion, Gwen and I will write those out and post, or hand deliver them today, so that will be one more post-it note for the recycling. Ophelia has got back to Lance about the band. She's in Aspen again at the moment but she'll make the necessary calls and has said that someone will contact me within a matter of days. If the band is good enough for Ophelia, I know it will be perfect as far as I'm concerned. So that makes three less things to worry about.

'Come on sleepy head,' Lance says, bringing me coffee and toast on a tray, in bed. 'Rise and shine. There's a big wide world out there and I'm sure someone somewhere needs help with their love life.'

I stretch and yawn then smile at him as I sit up.

'Nope. The only person's love life I'm interested in from now on, is my own. No more meddling for me.'

He puts the tray on the bedside table and sits on the edge of the bed.

'I love you exactly the way you are, Harriet. I told you that last night and I meant it. I don't want to change a thing about you. Not one thing. I think I simply worry that people might get hurt. You now know exactly what happened with Gwen and Jackson, and Merrion's filled me in this morning about what happened between her and Dan. Love is messy and complicated. Even more so when we don't know all the facts. But I know you mean well, and everything you do is with the best intentions, so I won't lecture you, or moan at you, or tell you what you should and shouldn't do. I'll let you work it out yourself.'

'I love you too. Exactly as you are. And I think, sometimes I could use a little advice. And possibly a little reminder that unicorns aren't real, the guy isn't always a prince and some princesses really don't need saving. They're perfectly capable of saving themselves.'

He smiles and kisses me and I think it might lead to a lot more than that until I hear Merrion shout from downstairs.

'Harri? Are you ever getting up? We've got things to do, places to go and people to see. Leave that man alone and get down here.'

Lance grins. 'I'd better go. Shall I come to yours tonight?'

'Yes.' I throw back the duvet and jump out of bed, pulling on my clothes whilst Lance watches me. 'And we'll continue exactly where we left off.' I smile and wink at him. 'I'll have a shower when I get home. I'd better not keep Merrion waiting. I'd completely forgotten she stayed here the night.'

'So had she!' He laughs. 'She came downstairs and her very words were: "Thank God it's you. When I woke up in a strange double bed, I thought I'd got drunk and hooked up with someone."'

'I wonder if she thought it was Dan.'

'Harriet. Unicorns and princes.' He tilts his head to one side and there's laughter in his eyes as well as in his voice.

'Damn. That didn't last long, did it?'

'I didn't think it would for one minute.'

'But you love me all the same.'

'Always. Now eat your toast.'

Merrion yells up the stairs again.

'We'll be celebrating *my* ninetieth birthday if you don't hurry up.'

Chapter Twenty-Six

They say time flies when you're having fun. It flies even faster when you're organising a ball.

It's June. It's raining. It's *been* raining for a week. An entire seven days. We now have small lakes where once there was lawn. There's so much mud out there we could probably make more money from music festivals or mud wrestling than we will from this ball. A ball, which is now less than two weeks away. And by the looks of things we stand a better chance of holding it on Mars than we do of dancing beneath a starlit sky. I'm considering changing the name to The Umbrella Ball.

But as Merrion keeps reminding me, I'm an unbridled optimist. At least I was. I'm trying very hard not to let this weather get me down. The good news is, most of the post-it notes now occupy the recycling bin.

We've met the members of the band Ophelia

recommended, and their repertoire is positively mind blowing. They can play any music we could ask for, with the possible exception of rap. Three of the members actually sneered when Gwen mentioned it and two of the others looked as if she had asked them to give her a lung or some other body part.

'I simply thought some of the younger people attending might like to hear one or two rap songs.'

'Think again,' Merrion said.

The best part is that Ophelia has insisted on paying their fees, and that's in addition to the fact that she is providing the flowers.

Our ball gowns have been altered. Not by Jodie's mum as it happens but by someone Ophelia's florist recommended. Susannah, the florist, came to discuss the floral arrangements just as Aunt Vicki was complaining about not being able to get staff these days.

'Seamstresses did *not* go off on last-minute holidays to Malaga in my day,' Aunt Vicki snapped.

'They probably hadn't heard of Malaga in your day,' Merrion said. 'And what's more, they were lucky if they got a half day off, let alone a holiday.'

Susannah caught my attention. 'Does your aunt need some dresses altered? Because if so, I happen to know someone who may be able to assist.'

'Oh. Are you by any chance related to my boyfriend, Lance?'

'Excuse me?' She was somewhat bewildered and, understandably hadn't got my joke.

'Sorry,' I said. 'Yes. We need five ball gowns altered. Nothing especially major, just a few nips and tucks.'

By then, Bella had also tried on one of Aunt Vicki's old gowns and found one she not only adored but that fitted to perfection – or would, once a couple of small panels of silk were added to each side. Apparently, baby-weight is harder to lose when you're fifty. Thankfully, the silk could be taken from the length. In her youth, Aunt Vicki had been taller than Bella. She had been taller than any of us. I'm not sure what we would have done had Aunt Vicki been diminutive in stature.

'I've got an idea,' Merrion says, joining Gwen, Bella and me in the kitchen. 'We could get Lance to build a couple of bridges, stick up a few poles and string lights around the lot. He's bound to know someone who could get his hands on a gondola or two. We could pretend the place is Venice.'

'I've never seen so much rain,' Gwen says. 'It's beginning to get on my nerves.'

'We certainly can't have marquees outside if the weather stays like this,' Bella adds. 'But do we have enough room to move the entire event inside?'

'If the RSVPs are any indication of attendance on the night,' I say, 'there's more than enough room inside. And we won't have to move a stick of furniture.'

'How many people are coming then?' Merrion asks.

'So far, Dad says we've sold ninety-five tickets.'

'Out of how many?'

'Three hundred and fifty. I knew we wouldn't sell them all but I was hoping for somewhere around the three hundred mark. Perhaps we're charging too much for the tickets.'

'Rubbish.' Merrion grabs some glasses and a bottle of wine. 'One hundred pounds for a ticket to *'A celebration of the birth of Lucinda Victoria Hall and to honour the ninetieth birthday of Victoria Elizabeth Margaret Fitzroy Hall'* is a snip. I paid almost twice that just for lunch in London the other day. Well, I didn't pay. My agent did. I think we may have made them too cheap. The more expensive something is, the more the punters want it.'

'And they are getting a crystal champagne flute commemorating the event to take home with them,' Bella says. 'I love the way Lucinda's name is written in a circle inside Vicki's.'

Gwen smiles. 'I hadn't realised Aunt Vicki had so many names when I suggested having them etched on the base, but it fits perfectly.'

Bella picks up a spare invitation from the box I've put on the table. 'I love these too. Especially the embossed drawing of Lucinda's hand in Vicki's. I've kept two to have framed as a gift for each of them. Thank you so much for that, sweetheart.' She squeezes my hand.

I smile at her. 'Lance knew an artist who copied it from a photo Dad took. So it really had very little to do with me.'

'It was your idea, so take the thanks,' Merrion says, pouring wine for the four of us. 'So what are we going to do to encourage people to come? Will we break even?'

'Yes. But only because Gwen here, and Lance and Ophelia seem to be paying for most of it. Without their generosity, we'd need to sell your new car.'

'It's for a good cause,' Gwen says. 'And we all love a birthday party.'

'Not everyone it seems,' says Merrion. 'At least not one they have to pay for.'

'There's still two weeks to go,' I say, 'Lots more people may RSVP between now and the 24th of June.'

'And if it doesn't stop raining, they'll have to swim to get here.'

'The worst part is I really wanted the Hall's Cross Animal Rescue Sanctuary to receive a substantial donation. Even though ninety per cent of the ticket price is going to the sanctuary, so far all they'll be receiving is enough to feed the animals, pay the staff and keep the lights on for a couple of weeks.'

'How much does it cost to keep the place going then?' Merrion asks. 'If we've sold ninety-five

tickets and they're getting ninety per cent that's…
well that's an awful lot of money for just a couple
of weeks.'

'There's rent and rates, water, gas, electricity,
vet's bills, medicines, food, bedding and toys for
the animals. Then there's telephone calls,
advertising, insurance.'

'Okay. I get the picture. How does the place
keep going?'

'With generous donations,' Bella says.

'Which at this rate,' I say, 'they won't be
getting from us.'

'They damn well will,' Merrion says.

She has a determined look on her face and for a
fleeting moment, I wonder if she's actually
considering selling her new car and donating the
money to the sanctuary.

'Are you planning to rally the troops?' Bella
asks.

'I'm planning to contact everyone I know in
the fashion and modelling business. They've all
got a few pounds they can spare for a good cause.
In fact…'

'Yes…?' I say. I can tell from her eyes that
she's excited.

She shakes her head. 'No. I'm not going to say
anything until it's definite, but I've just had a
rather good idea.'

'I hope it's better than your last one. As much
as I love Venice, that simply wouldn't work.'

'Oh, it's much, much better than that. And I'm

pretty certain this one will work. I need to make some calls. I'll be back later.'

She refills her glass and dashes out of the kitchen with it, sending droplets of white wine splashing over the rim and onto the floor.

'Merrion seems excited,' Gwen says.

'Yes,' says Bella, smiling. 'Other than when we brought Lucinda home, I haven't seen my daughter that excited for some considerable time.'

I sincerely hope her idea pans out. It's good to see Merrion excited about something again.

Chapter Twenty-Seven

'You've done what?' I ask, unable to believe what Merrion's just told us, especially as it's only about three hours or so since she left us.

'I've arranged a photo shoot at the Hall's Cross Animal Rescue Sanctuary. But I need you to tell Dan because I don't want to have anything to do with him. You can tell him it was your idea. We simply need the sanctuary's permission. My friends and colleagues will sort everything out.'

'What type of photo shoot is it going to be?' Gwen asks. 'Will it involve the animals?'

'Completely. We're not planning to dress them up exactly, but we're going to have them wearing jewellery, and fascinators, scarves, and such. You know. A sort of Cinderella storyline. Rags to riches and all that. We'll have them groomed and coiffed to within an inch of their furry little lives. There will be before and after photos. And they'll be posed with models of course, possibly in the animals' cages – but that depends on the cages – or whatever it is they're housed in. There's already one well-known fashion mag interested, a high-end store, a jewellery designer who sells to A-list celebrities and a photographer whose photographs sell for thousands of pounds a time. Everyone we've spoken to so far is willing to give their time and expertise for free, and to donate a large portion of any profits. If that doesn't make tens of thousands, then nothing will.'

Now I really can't believe it. 'And you've managed to arrange all this in only a couple of hours? Wow, Merrion. You should get excited about things more often. That's incredible.'

'It won't happen for a while. It takes time to organise diaries. But at least it's got the green light. And if something happens and it doesn't go ahead for whatever reason, the people I've spoken to will still donate several thousand pounds. I know them personally and once they say they'll do something, they do it. So either way, the sanctuary will be able to count on some extra funds heading in its direction in the not too distant future. And it should be enough to keep the place open for months, if not years.'

'It's brilliant,' I say, 'but it really should be you who tells Dan, not me.'

'No!' Merrion says. 'I'm doing this for the animals, not for him. I don't want him to think I'm trying to get him to sleep with me out of gratitude or something.'

'What! Bella says, completely unaware of the

history between Merrion and Dan. 'Why on earth would he think that?'

'Oh. Um. Because he's a man, Mum. All men think that way.'

'Not the men I know, darling.'

'Well, that's because you don't know Dan.'

'No. I haven't met him yet. But I shall when we finally go to the sanctuary to look at some dogs to adopt.'

'You're not still seriously considering that, are you?' Merrion asks. 'Haven't you got enough to cope with?'

Bella smiles. 'I can't seem to get the idea out of my head. I have visions of the twins playing nicely with them in the garden. Of Reece training them. The dogs that is, not the twins. Of Vicki carrying her little dog under her arm. It all seems so perfect.'

'Really?' Merrion says. 'I have visions of Reece blowing his dog sky high, the twins training theirs to be attack dogs, and Aunt Vicki's dog to be even grumpier than she is and to snap people's fingers off when they try to stroke it. That's not counting the piles of poo all over the house, the smell of wet dog – in more ways than one, and we mustn't forget the barking and howling we'll have to put up with all through the night. Oh, wait. We've got that already with Lucinda.'

Bella laughs and hugs Merrion. 'Oh darling, you do make me laugh. Maybe we should get a dog for you too.'

'Don't even think about it,' Merrion says. 'I'll move out if you do.'

Chapter Twenty-Eight

'Look, Lance,' I say, pointing up at the white and green Hall's Cross Animal Rescue Sanctuary sign as we drive into the car park. 'It reads as 'Animal' again. I assume you got that man you know to fix it.'

'Yep. And he did it for just the price of the materials. Or I suppose I should say, letters, in this case.'

'Thanks for coming with me. I wish I could've persuaded Merrion, but she was adamant that there was no way she wanted to see Dan's face at the moment. I think she may still be a little in love with him, you know. She says she isn't of course, and after he walked away without so much as a goodbye, who can blame her, but I can tell she feels something for him. If she didn't, it wouldn't bother her to see him, would it? Lance?'

'Yes, Harriet?'

'Did you hear what I said?'

'Yes, Harriet.'

'And…?'

'And it sounded very much like unicorns and princes to me.'

I shift a little uncomfortably in the seat of Lance's truck. He's right. I'm meddling again. Even if it is only in thought.

'I'm not going to meddle, Lance. Cross my heart.'

He grins as we get out of the truck. 'We'll see.'

'No really. I won't. Oh. Who's that girl with Dan? They look very…' I let my voice trail off.

I'm doing it again. But I can see Dan standing at the door of his cottage talking to a woman with long chestnut-coloured hair. And they look rather friendly with one another. I glance at my watch and see it's not yet nine. The sanctuary doesn't open until nine. Either this woman is early and called at the cottage as the sanctuary was closed. Or she is leaving the cottage. Which can only mean one thing: The woman with chestnut-coloured hair is the girlfriend Dan told us he was going to be seeing again.

'Hi, Dan.'

I call and wave but he's already seen us. He gives the woman what looks like a bunch of keys and hurries towards me and Lance.

'Hello, Harriet. Hi, Lance. It's good to see you again. Have you come about the dog, Harriet?'

'Er. No. And we may not be getting one dog now.'

'I'm sorry to hear that, but I understand completely. People often change their minds. Better now than after they've taken the animal home with them. It's unsettling for any animal to go back and forth. It's not a problem. Thanks for letting me know.'

I wag my finger at him. 'Tut-tut, Dan. You jumped in whilst I was taking a breath. We may not be getting *one* dog now. We may be getting four dogs.'

Dan blinks several times. 'I'm sorry. Did you just say that you may want four dogs? Four?'

I nod. 'One for Aunt Vicki. One for my stepbrother Reece. And one each for the terrible… I mean, the twins. Theo and Thor. You've met Reece, but you've yet to have the pleasure of coming face to face with my darling little twin brothers.'

'And it *will* be a pleasure, Dan,' Lance says, grinning. 'Believe me.'

'Hmm. From what the staff here tell me, young Theo and Thor may have been the ones who let the dogs and the rest of the animals out.'

'Very possibly,' I say. 'Um. We're not keeping you from your… friend, are we? I think she's waiting for you. Would you like us to come back later? Is this an inconvenient time?'

Lance tuts and takes my hand in his but doesn't say a word. Dan looks back at the chestnut-haired woman who is looking up at the cottage as if she doesn't know where else to look.

'No,' Dan says, without the slightest hint of embarrassment or concern. 'She's fine. So have you come to choose four dogs today then? There are a couple of forms we need to fill in and I do have to do a home check. Sorry, it's procedure. But you can definitely have a look today.'

'Thanks, but Bella wants to come with Dad and have a look and then if that's okay with you, come back with the twins and Reece.'

'That's fine. So if it's not about the dogs, I assume it must be about The Starlight Ball. How are things going with that? Is there anything you need me to do? Other than buy a ticket, that is. And, as it happens, I need to talk to you about that.'

'Oh. The cost you mean? Don't worry about that. You don't need to pay.'

He looks confused. 'No. Not the cost. I'm happy to pay. That's not the problem. It's your sister.'

'Merrion?'

Lance squeezes my hand. 'What's the problem with Merrion?' he asks.

Now Dan does look both embarrassed and concerned.

'I'm not sure if you're aware of this but Merrion and I have met before.'

'Yes. She told us.'

'Oh. Then I'm sure you can understand why I'd rather not attend unless it's absolutely necessary.'

'Merrion's a big girl, Dan.' I try to keep the

note of censure from my voice but I know I'm failing miserably. 'Just because you spent the night with her and left in the morning without a word doesn't mean you can't attend the ball. I'm sure she doesn't hold it against you.'

Lance sighs. 'Actually she does. And so would most women. I'm sorry, Harriet. There's no point in lying. But your love life's your business, Dan. This is about the animals.'

'I'm sorry. What?' Dan looks even more confused.

'The sanctuary. We've come to run an idea by you.'

'Wait. Go back a step. What did you say about Merrion not holding it against me?'

Lance tuts. 'I said she *does* hold it against you.'

I stare at Lance in disbelief. 'Now who's interfering in someone's love life?'

'I'm not interfering. I'm simply telling the truth.'

'And the difference is…?'

'Hold on,' Dan says. 'What did you say? Not that bit. The other bit. The bit about me leaving without a word. That sounds as if I used her and walked away. I didn't. I left word. Several words. It was Merrion who did the walking.'

Lance and I look at one another and then at Dan.

'That's not what Merrion says,' I tell him.

'Well, if you want the truth. I've told the truth. I was nuts about your sister from the minute she spilt her drink on me to the minute her assistant told me Merrion was as good as living with an exceedingly wealthy, older guy, but that she likes the occasional session with a 'young bit of rough'. And you know what? I was still nuts about her. Her assistant told me to leave and not to cause a scene. So I left. But I left my number and a note virtually begging Merrion to call me even though I was also told if I didn't have money I should forget it. And I haven't the faintest idea why I've just told you all that.'

'Dan?' The woman with the chestnut hair is calling him and he turns and marches towards her.

'What just happened?' I look at Lance and see that he's as astonished as me.

He shakes his head. 'I'm not completely sure, but I think Dan just told us that Merrion's assistant is what Gwen would call 'a first-class bitch'. And I think the sooner we tell Merrion that, the better. I also think Dan may well be in love with your sister.'

'I absolutely agree. But there's just one tiny problem.'

Lance gives a strange little laugh. 'Just the one?'

I nod my head in the direction of the woman with chestnut hair. 'Dan now has a girlfriend and he has given her keys to his house, which means it's pretty serious.'

'How do you know that?'

'Because I saw him give them to her when we

161

arrived.'

'Oh. In that case I think we'd better ask him?'

'What happened to not interfering? Sorry. Just saying.'

'This is the exception to the rule.'

Dan saunters back towards us with his hands stuffed in his pockets, his shoulders hunched and an oddly embarrassed expression on his face.

'So what is this idea you want to talk about?'

'We'll get to that in a minute,' I say, cutting to the chase. 'Is your girlfriend moving in with you?'

'My what?'

'Your girlfriend.' I nod towards the woman who is still looking up at the thatched roof. 'She either really likes that roof, or else she really hates it.'

Dan busts out laughing. 'I think it's a mixture of both. That's Jeanette. She's not my girlfriend. I don't have a girlfriend. I went out on a date but… Well, that doesn't matter. Jeanette's a thatcher. She's come to repair the roof.

Chapter Twenty-Nine

'What's this about?' Merrion asks me when I call her on the phone. 'Why the urgency? I'm still in bed. I didn't get hardly any sleep last night and I'm absolutely shattered. Why do you need to come and pick me up and take me to see someone? Who? Oh, God. This isn't one of your matchmaking schemes, is it? Because I'm not interested. I thought I made that clear.'

'I told you,' I say. 'It's about your assistant. Not that I knew you had an assistant.'

'I don't.'

That comes as a surprise. 'You don't?'

'No.'

'But... you must have.'

'Believe me, Harri, that's what I keep saying. But it falls on deaf ears.'

'So... who books your hotel rooms? Who knows details of your life? The people you see? Stuff like that?' I can hear her yawn and I wait impatiently for her reply.

'God. I don't know. What's this about? My agent deals with most of it. The magazines' staff, or the photographers or whoever I'm working for on a particular assignment, I suppose. I'm too tired to think. Why do you want to know? Is this about the photo shoot at the animal sanctuary or something?' She yawns again. 'I need sleep. Can we talk about this later?'

She rings off before I get a chance to say another word.

I look at Lance and shake my head. 'She needs to sleep, apparently. I think the best way to handle this is to take Dan to The Hall. I'd have to lie to get her here and she'd be so cross that she wouldn't listen to anyone anyway.'

'But would Dan go?'

Dan is currently dealing with a dog with an upset tummy so we can't ask him in person. We are sitting in his tiny office, drinking the coffee he told us to make as he went off to handle the situation.

'Yes, I think so. You saw his face when I told him that Merrion wasn't living with anyone. Other than our family, of course.'

'I also saw his face when you added the fact that she did have a very rich, older friend, who sometimes buys her presents.'

'But I made it clear they were merely friends.'

'Abundantly. Although I'm not sure repeating the same sentence several times actually makes it any clearer. He didn't look that convinced to me.'

'Do you think he'll be long?'

'I think it depends just how upset that poor dog's tummy is. But I suspect Dan wouldn't want to leave in any case. This is his job, after all. I don't think he would be inclined to tell the animals to look after themselves while he sorts out his love life.'

'He's got staff.'

'I still don't think he'd go. And I can't stick around for much longer. I told my guys I'd be on site by ten. Why don't we leave it for now? If Merrion doesn't have an assistant, we have no idea who talked to Dan. She'd have to know who was in her hotel room that morning. That may be simple or it may not.'

'I've just had an idea. Why don't we ask Bella if we can invite Dan round for dinner? We can tell him it's to discuss the ball and also what we came here to discuss originally. I'll say that Merrion's not going to be there. All we need to do is to get them in a room together and get them talking.'

'That's a possibility. It might work. Okay, let's give it a try.'

I immediately phone Bella and, without giving her all the details, ask if Dan can join us for dinner tonight. She's naturally a bit reluctant at first, knowing that Merrion can't seem to abide the man, but when I assure her that it has all been a silly misunderstanding, which can be put right in a matter of a ten-minute conversation, providing we can get Dan and Merrion together in the same room, she agrees. Bella dislikes unpleasantness of any kind. She's one of the world's born peacekeepers. I'm sure The United Nations would be thrilled to have her on their staff if she ever wanted to apply.

'You're certain about this, sweetheart?' she asks.

'One hundred and ten per cent,' I say. 'Dan's just filled us in on his side of the story and it seems that someone who works with Merrion may not have her best interests at heart. Don't you think the sooner she knows about it, the better?'

'Oh, good gracious. Who is this person? Do we have a name?'

'No. But Dan can describe the person and answer any questions Merrion may have, which would be far easier if they were face to face.'

'And… after that, Merrion won't detest Daniel quite so much, is that what you're saying?'

'Yes. In fact, I think once she's heard what Dan's got to say, she may actually like him. She may like him a lot.'

'Well in that case, yes of course he must come to dinner. I'll have to see what we have in the fridge. I may need to send Ralph out for supplies.'

'It doesn't need to be anything special. I'm hoping the food will be the last thing on their minds once they've had time to talk.'

'Oh, but sweetheart, we can hardly invite a guest for dinner and give him beans on toast.'

'I don't know. Beans on toast might very well

be Dan's favourite dish.'

Bella gives a little gurgle of laughter. Or it may possibly have been Lucinda, suffering from wind.

'I think we can do a little better than that, can't we, darling?' Bella says.

I'm not sure if she's talking to me or the baby, so I say: 'Great. I'll see you later. Text me if there's anything you need.' I hang up and it's perfect timing. Dan is returning to his office.

'How's the dog?' Lance asks.

'He'll be okay. I don't think it's anything serious but we'll call the vet if he doesn't perk up.'

'That's good news,' I say, getting to my feet. 'You're obviously extremely busy, so we'll get out of your hair.' Lance stands up but gives me a questioning look, as does Dan.

'Er. Didn't you come here to tell me something?'

'Yes. But it can wait. Do you have dinner plans tonight?'

'Tonight?'

'Yes.'

'No. No plans. I was going to the pub for a pie and a pint.'

'Perfect,' I say. 'Bella wants you to join us for dinner tonight. At The Hall. And before you say no, Merrion won't be there.'

'She won't? Oh.' He actually sounds disappointed.

'No. She's busy.'

'Oh.'

167

'So will you come? Everyone wants to meet you. Shall we say seven-thirty for eight?'

'Um. Yeah. Yes, of course. Thanks. I'd love to meet the rest of the family. Is that what you both came here to ask me? I thought you mentioned something about an idea.'

I hesitate. I don't want to tell him about Merrion's photo shoot now because it will sound so much better coming from her. Thankfully, Lance steps in.

'That was it. Bella and Wyndham thought it would be a good idea to meet you, bearing in mind The Starlight Ball is at their home and you're the manager of the sanctuary.'

'Yes,' I add. 'And it'll also give them a chance to discuss the possibility of the family adopting four dogs. Plus it would give you an opportunity to look the place over and see if it's okay. You said you'd need to do a home check. What better way to check a home than by going there for dinner?'

He still looks a little bewildered but he slowly nods his head.

'Okay then. I guess that means I'll see you around seven-thirty. Thanks.'

'Thank you,' I say. 'You have no idea how much we're already looking forward to it. Now we have to dash. Lance is late for work and I have a million things still to do to finalise The Starlight Ball.'

Chapter Thirty

'Something smells nice,' Merrion says, coming into the kitchen where I'm checking on dinner whilst Bella and everyone else is getting ready. 'So what did you say we're celebrating?'

I feel a touch guilty for lying to Merrion but I had to tell her we were having a celebratory dinner or she would have worn her usual casual clothes. Merrion looks good no matter what she wears, but tonight I wanted her to look extra special... because tonight Dan is coming to dinner.

I'm not sure how I convinced her but Lance suggested I say that we're celebrating the fact that Gwen has decided it's time she moved on from Jackson Hunter, and Merrion actually believed it.

And it wasn't a complete lie. Gwen has decided that. After seeing him on TV that night in the pub and filling us in on exactly what happened, Gwen said she really needed to 'get over it. To finally get over *him*,' and she's doing rather well. Ralph's been helping by spending time with her.

Now she may be able to return the favour. When I got home today Ralph told us the latest news. It seems Jodie's boyfriend decided he wanted her back, so unfortunately, Ralph is now history as far as Jodie is concerned.

Aunt Vicki says the wretched girl used him to make her ex-boyfriend jealous, and we think she may be right. But we haven't said that to Ralph. No one likes the thought of being a pawn in someone else's game of love.

But Ralph doesn't seem that bothered. I don't think he would have told us all if he was. He would have kept it to himself. Ralph's good at keeping his own secrets. It's other people's he tends to share without a second thought.

And it means that Ralph won't be spending so much time in the pub, and that's a very good thing. Plus he and Gwen have always got on well. Merrion says they hit it off the very first time they met. But then Ralph gets on with everyone. He's so laid back and easy going. Possibly a bit too laid back at times. But the important thing is, he and Gwen can heal each other's broken hearts. So now all we have to do is sort out Merrion's. And by the night of The Starlight Ball, Gwen and Ralph may each be ready to fall in love with someone new. Things are working out rather well. Although not quite as I had planned.

'We're celebrating Gwen's fresh start,' I remind Merrion. She was still half asleep when I told her this morning. She didn't get up until two this afternoon and I was worried she would still look shattered tonight. But Merrion can look good even when she's tired, unlike me.

'Perhaps we should be celebrating Ralph's fresh start too. Thank God he's no longer with Jodie.'

'Yes. But as he only told us that this afternoon, I think it may be a bit too soon for him to celebrate, don't you?'

Merrion shrugs. 'Perhaps. But he didn't bat an eye when Dad came back from his last minute shopping trip to the village and said that he'd bumped into Jodie. She had asked after Ralph, apparently, because she wanted to check he was okay.'

'How considerate of her,' I say, somewhat sarcastically.

'Dad thought it was, but you know Dad. He assured her Ralph was fine. Anyway, when he told Ralph that she'd been worried about him, Ralph replied: "That's sweet of her," and not sarcastically as you and I have. He genuinely meant it. Just like Dad did. Then Ralph carried on with what he was doing as if Dad hadn't mentioned Jodie at all.'

'That's good. And whatever he's doing with Gwen is clearly working. I've never seen her as happy as she's been for the last few days.'

'Yes clearly,' Merrion says. 'And I think we may need to talk about that.'

'Oh? That sounds a bit odd. What's wrong?' I wipe my hands on a tea towel and turn to face her.

She looks me up and down. 'Is that what you're wearing tonight? I thought you said we should all get dressed up?'

'Oh shit!' I dash towards the door just as Bella is coming in. 'I'm just going to get changed, Bella. Dinner's nearly ready. We'll be back before you know it.'

Bella smiles and shakes her head. 'You're cutting things a bit fine, sweetheart.'

'I know. Merrion, come upstairs with me and tell me what you were going to say. We don't have much time before Dan... I mean Dad. Before Dad will be rounding us all up for dinner.'

'Did you just say Dan?' she asks, following me into the Great Hall.

'It was a slip of the tongue. He was on my mind because I saw him today. Lance and I went to tell him about your photo shoot.'

She rushes to my side. 'Oh? How did he take it?'

We're now running up the stairs as the rest of my family are starting to walk down them.

'Where are you two off to in such a hurry? Dad asks, stepping to one side.

'I need to get changed,' I say.

'I'm going to help her,' Merrion says as we both race past him. 'So tell me then. How did he take it?'

'Um. He didn't. That is, we didn't get a chance to tell him. The thatcher was there and one of the dogs had an upset tummy. It didn't seem quite the right time.'

I hear the doorbell ring and I freeze on the spot just a few stairs from the top. Merrion stops too but she's giving me a very odd look; as if to say: 'It's the doorbell, what's the problem? Is there a problem?' She doesn't say anything, though. She merely looks at me and then glances towards the door.

But when the front door swings open one second later, I realise it's Lance and Gwen and I breathe a sigh of relief.

My relief is short-lived. Dan walks in right behind them. I hear Merrion gasp as she grips my forearm.

'What in God's name is he doing here!' she shrieks, staring at Dan.

Dan's mouth falls open but he quickly recovers himself. 'What am I doing here? What are you doing here?'

'I live here. Who invited you?' She turns and glowers at me. 'Harriet? Does this have anything to do with you because if it does you won't live to see your precious Starlight Ball.' And she tightens her grip on my arm.

'Now stop this at once,' Bella demands from the kitchen doorway. 'Merrion. I believe you and Daniel need to talk.'

'I have nothing to say to him,' Merrion says through gritted teeth, all the while staring at me as if she would like to burn me alive.'

'I'm not rich enough for her to bother with,'

Dan hisses. And that's odd because he doesn't strike me as a petulant man.

'What?' Merrion now turns her fiery stare back to him. 'What has money got to do with anything?'

'Quite a lot as far as you're concerned. How much do I have to have to get you to give me the time of day?'

'What are you ranting about? You don't need money. I'm not interested in money. I don't give a damn how much you have.'

'Please!' Bella shouts. 'Stop this.' She sounds as if she may burst into tears. That shuts Merrion up immediately. She lets go of me and rushes down the stairs to her mum.

Dad's already got there and he wraps his arms around Bella. Aunt Vicki appears from the sitting room and rapidly takes in the scene. Ralph goes to stand near Gwen and Lance and Dan takes a few steps forward, then stops as if he's not sure what he should do. Reece wanders past me down the stairs and doesn't even notice what's going on. His head is buried in his iPad and I wonder if he'll make it down the stairs without falling, but then as this is his semi-permanent state, I know full well he'll be fine. I just stay where I am. I want to go and change but I don't want to miss anything.

'I'm sorry, Mum,' Merrion says, as she reaches Bella's side. 'Are you okay? Let's go and sit down.'

'I don't want to sit down,' Bella says. 'I want the two of you to have a conversation. Harri assured me all you needed to do was talk. So please, my darling, talk to him.'

'I'm sorry if I upset you, Mrs Hall,' Dan says, looking considerably calmer than he had. 'I don't know what Harriet has said but I'm perfectly willing to have a conversation with Merrion if it helps.'

'You can go and use Wyndham's study,' Aunt Vicki offers without first checking with Dad.

'They can?' Dad says. 'Oh yes. Of course you can, Merrion. Go to my study and have a chat. We'll hold dinner for you, won't we darling? And Reece, where are those cocktails you usually make?'

Reece glances up from his iPad at the mention of his name. 'There's a jug in the fridge,' he says. 'I made them earlier today.'

'Well, give Merrion and Daniel some of those and bring ours into the sitting room, please, there's a good lad. I'd better just pop upstairs and take a peek at Lucinda and the twins. Make sure none of this has woken them.'

'Believe me, Dad,' I say, 'if Lucinda and the twins were awake, we'd all know about it.' Merrion glares at me again. 'But let me nip upstairs and check for you. I'm halfway there already.' I turn on my heel and dash up the stairs. From here on in, Merrion and Dan are on their own as far as I'm concerned.

Chapter Thirty-One

I don't know if the cocktails helped but when I come back downstairs, everyone is in the sitting room and most of them are smiling. Everyone except Dan and Merrion that is, who must still be in Dad's study. I'm a little disappointed that it seems to be taking them so long to talk things through but on the other hand, I'm glad I haven't missed anything. When they finally reappear ten minutes after me, not only are they smiling, they're actually standing side by side and I'm almost certain their fingers are touching. But that may be wishful thinking on my part.

'Everything sorted?' I ask, as they stand in the doorway.

Merrion nods. 'Almost everything.' She looks up at Dan and if that's not a look of love, then I don't know what love is. 'Apart from the fact that I need to have a word with a certain photographer's assistant.'

'A photographer's assistant? Is that who she

was? Why does she have it in for you?'

Merrion shakes her head. 'I'm not sure she does. I think she may have simply been telling Dan what she considers to be the facts. She's seen me with my friend, Constantine many, many times and although I can promise you he and I have never been anything but good friends, Cheryl – that's her name – may well have misinterpreted the situation.'

'I think you may be giving her the benefit of the doubt,' I say.

'Possibly. Once I've spoken to her I'll know for sure. But I genuinely thought we got on. She's always doing me favours whenever she's on one of our shoots. She was actually doing me a favour that day, although I didn't know it. I couldn't find my phone and mentioned I must've left in my room. I was planning to get it… and to nip back and see Dan… as soon as the meeting to discuss the shoot was over. By the time it was, my phone was sitting on top of my bag and when I went up to my room to see Dan, he had gone.'

'But that doesn't explain why she said such horrible things. I mean, telling a guy that you like a bit of… um… like to see other men even when you're supposedly living with someone, isn't something you want your so-called friends to be saying about you, is it?' I have to be careful what I say. Dad, Bella and the rest of the family are listening, after all.

'Well no. I suppose not. But, as I said, perhaps

that *is* how she sees me. A spoilt, and she probably believes, rich, model being showered with gifts by an older man and spending the night with a gorgeous young man. She obviously doesn't know the real me. And that's my fault. I need her to see who I really am.'

'If you say so.' I'm not convinced, but it's up to Merrion how she handles this.

'Of course,' Merrion says, with a grin. 'If she still says horrid things, she'll soon find out just how spoilt and unpleasant I can be.'

'And that's not a pretty sight,' says Ralph.

Dan looks into Merrion's eyes. 'I don't believe that for a moment.'

'Does this mean we can finally eat?' Aunt Vicki says. 'I'm almost ninety, you know, young man. I need to keep up my strength.'

Chapter Thirty-Two

Love is a very funny thing. It's often unexpected; sometimes it's a complete surprise. Often it's a shock. It frequently turns up in the last place we would ever think to look and often when we would rather it didn't. But that's what makes Love so exciting. And our lives are always better if we have a little Love in them.

It doesn't need to be Love for another human being, of course. It can be Love for anything. Love for life itself. And there's something very special about the Love we feel for our pets.

Today is Aunt Vicki's ninetieth birthday. It's also the evening of The Starlight Ball. I think it's going to be perfect. I know it's going to be a success. Nothing can ruin it now. Even the weather has decided to do its best for us. It is for a good cause, after all. It hasn't rained for days and the ground has finally dried out.

We've even managed to get the marquees we were hoping for. Although we did have to get some more to cater for the number of guests we're expecting. Luckily, Lance knew a man who could help, which is just as well. The number of RSVPs hit three hundred and fifty the day after Merrion made her telephone calls about the photo shoot and word got around the village faster than the speed of light. Since then we've had a further three hundred invitations printed and accepted and so many more enquiries and requests, it will take us a month of Sundays to reply to them all.

I'd like to say that it's all due to my superb organisation skills but the fact of the matter is the success of The Starlight Ball will have very little to do with me. It has a great deal to do with my wonderful family, my boyfriend's wonderful family, and my gorgeous boyfriend too. Not forgetting Merrion's equally gorgeous boyfriend, Dan, and Merrion's friends and contacts.

It's even been suggested that we might like to start a new venture. The Hall is the perfect setting for a ball. For any ball. And balls are big business so it seems. But I'm not sure we want that. Dad said no to my ex-boyfriend's mother's TV cookery show being filmed here. I don't think he really wants hundreds of people dancing in the Great Hall or in the grounds on a regular basis either. And Aunt Vicki moans about the few paying visitors who come to see the kitchen and scullery. The one that's the best preserved example of a late fifteenth-early sixteenth-century kitchen in the whole of England. Although since Reece blew part of it up before I came home last year, some of it is no longer as original as it looks, and some of it isn't even that ancient as Lance couldn't source replacements parts so reproductions had to do. Not that anyone seems to have noticed.

Besides, money isn't everything.

But Dad has agreed that The Hall can appear in a second photo shoot. The one for the sanctuary is due to take place at the end of June but during discussions with Merrion, one magazine editor saw some pictures of The Hall and fell in love with it. So The Hall is going to be the back drop for their Christmas cover and a five page spread. It's taking place in July so that should be interesting. Reece is already seeing if he can make his own artificial snow.

The Starlight Ball will also be a success because of Ophelia and her contacts. And in no small way, because of Lance and all the people he knows.

But mainly it will be because of Gwen. Not only is she completely over Jackson Hunter; she has beaten him to the punch. With considerable help from Ralph, she has written a book in just two weeks. Admittedly, it's a short book but I think it may well be this year's bestseller.

Her soon to be self-published memoir: *The Knightly-Hunter Diaries* has hit number one with pre-orders on every single site where it's available and it's only been available for three days. Publishers are clamouring for the hardback and paperback rights already. There's even talk of a film.

When Gwen announced her book to the world via the tiny local paper, the Hall's Cross Weekly News, the interview went viral. And because she mentioned The Starlight Ball and that all the proceeds from the ball and the sale of her book will be donated to the Hall's Cross Animal Rescue Sanctuary, tickets became like gold bars. Everyone wanted one. And everyone wanted the book. A lot of people want to adopt the animals at the sanctuary too. Dan says the phone's been ringing off the hook.

So everyone is happy. Well, almost everyone. I'm a bit worried about Ralph.

As I stand at the open front doors of The Hall beneath the colonnade strewn with fairy lights and look down the drive lit by flickering flames in wrought iron torches, I wonder how things will turn out.

Lance hugs me tightly to him. 'What's going on in that head of yours?'

There's so much love in his eyes I feel as if I might burst. I take two deep breaths and tell him.

'It's Ralph and Gwen.'

He glances around as if expecting to see them but I know they're in the sitting room with Aunt Vicki and the Yorkshire terrier she's adopted via a birthday present from me.

'What's Ralph and Gwen? Do you mean that's who's on your mind? Your brother and my sister.

Why now?'

I look into his eyes and all I see is happiness.

'They've become virtually inseparable. Haven't you noticed?'

He smiles. 'I'm not blind. Why, is that a problem?'

'I'm not sure you understand. They're not just friends now, Lance. I think… I think it's more than that. I think… they may be in love. Or they think they are.'

'And…?'

'Doesn't that bother you?'

'No. Okay. I'll admit it did a little at first. But when I saw how happy Gwen is, how happy they both are. No. Are you saying it bothers you?'

'A little, yes.'

'Why? Because you think Gwen might flip again and hit your brother with a pan or something? I don't think she will. I'm positive she won't, in fact. Nothing like that will ever happen again, Harriet. I'm willing to stake my life on that. And Ralph's not Jackson Hunter.'

'I didn't even think about Gwen and the pan. That's not what worries me. Gwen's eighteen. Ralph's my age. That's a twelve-year difference.'

'So what?'

'So what! Twelve years, Lance. That's a lot'

He smiles and pushes a wisp of hair from my face. 'Only in numbers. Age doesn't matter, Harriet. Not when Love is concerned. And besides, Ralph doesn't act like a thirty-year-old man and since Gwen's been with Ralph, she doesn't act like a teenager. I think they're good for one another. They like the same things. They make each other laugh. Surely that's what matters?'

'So you're happy that they're together.'

'If they're happy, then yes. I couldn't ask for a better man than Ralph to be with my baby sister.'

He's right of course. But then he always is. So I forget about Gwen and Ralph and think instead about how completely wonderful The Starlight Ball is going to be. The marquees in the back garden are hung with fragrant flowers and twinkling fairy lights. And stunning displays of flowers, from brightly coloured Strelitzia – birds of paradise as they're known – to Anthurium and Lilies to simpler Daisies and Roses, adorn every room in The Hall and fill them with heady scents. Mingled with the aromas wafting from the kitchen and the dining room, the perfume each of our guests will be wearing will have stiff competition.

The band is warming up and melodious notes from The Moonlight Sonata drift towards us through the air. Lance holds me tighter in his arms and gently sways me from side to side.

'Happy?' he asks.

'Blissfully,' I reply.

And when he kisses me, I know that tonight will go off without a hitch. That no animals will run riot. That the twins who have been allowed to stay up for the first hour of the ball will behave. That Lucinda will be the perfect, peacefully sleeping baby. That Aunt Vicki will proudly parade her new pet dog – whose name is Harry, with a 'y', as it's a male – to and fro. That Bella and Dad, Merrion and Dan, Gwen and Ralph and Lance and I will all be blissfully happy. And hopefully, not just for tonight, but for many, many more nights and years to come.

I also know that darling Reece will not blow anything up tonight, because he's far too busy researching 'Dog Training' on his iPad these days in preparation for when we adopt the other three dogs. Although his interest in making artificial snow may cause a bit of a blip for a short time. But definitely not tonight. Tonight will be a perfect night.

And I don't need to wish upon one of the myriad shining stars above us to know that. I know it in my heart.

The End

Thank you for reading, *The Starlight Ball*. I hope you enjoyed it and if so, I would absolutely love it if you would tell your friends and/or post a short review on Amazon. Word of mouth is an author's best friend and very much appreciated. Thanks a million.

To see details of my other books, please go to the books page on my website or scan the QR code, below. www.emilyharvale.com/books.

***

Scan the code above to see Emily's books on Amazon

To read about me, my books, my work in progress and competitions, freebies, or to contact me, pop over to my website www.emilyharvale.com. To be the first to hear about new releases and other news, you can subscribe to my Readers' Club newsletter via the 'Sign me up' box.
Or come and say 'Hello' on Facebook, Twitter, Instagram or Pinterest. Hope to chat with you soon.

Printed in Great Britain
by Amazon